THE BURNING BUSH WOMEN
&
OTHER STORIES

CHERIE JONES

THE BURNING BUSH WOMEN
&
OTHER STORIES

PEEPAL TREE

First published in Great Britain in 2004
Peepal Tree Press Ltd
17 King's Avenue
Leeds LS6 1QS
England

ISBN 1 900715 58 9

 Peepal Tree gratefully acknowledges Arts Council support

HAIR

sssSsssssssss

is the alaric androgynous lair from which these sweet flat black
woman poems *sally* forth to sack Rome. to recover the swamps and
the swollen stolen provin- ces of our what people are calling *'post-
colon ial literature'* which is literature that is being asked to forget &
even forgive its origins in take-over & under -throw. in savage & light
night. where gender meant harsh not tender xplosure. where the
women of these poems wd have been left sucking salt in the salvages

but not here . not here. where *flat* means just what it seems like -
difference - dissonace - the flattened seventh - berg - bela bartok
- thelonious monk - el verno del congo - that sound of silence after
the fire-begrade has pass(ed) into the *futu* future. *ending with as
many Questions as it began*

which is why *We live by our hair -*

haven't heard that one before. have you! tho even before this -
dorothea smartt - there were these *medusa poems*. So at least
there's been some warning. But not this storm -

*We welcome rain when our plaits undo of their own volition and retreat
into them selves. We are pregnant when our hair turns the colour of
beetroot and are about to die when it lies still against our scalps and
becomes straight and starts to drain itself of its fire. We are sick when it
refuses to be ignited by sunlight.*

A few years ago - in 1999 - again w/out warning and I suspect
largely unsus- pected ignored - like the creative terrorist of new

metaphor that she is - tho she'll say No - tho she'll demur - and she's also a corporate law lawyer after all - tho I suspect she's about to leave all that behind - these poems - I call these stories poems - are too maroon - too GrandeeNanny to remain in CBC in CBS -

so in 1999. the Commonwealth Broadcasting Association - the CBA - in associ- ation w/the BBC itself. in their great international shortstory competition. sel- ects THE BRIDE as unanimous NO 1 - that year's cynosure out of almost 5000 aspirators. But many miss that then (and the CD that goes w/the winning) tho thank- fully its here again - one more bottle of omen on the Peepal Tree of the People

'The Bride' is an ambush - Burning Bush Women is not an accidental title. is what peepal call *xponitential.* All this potential penitential. And still more meanings throng in natural - penis - penal - protein - protean - *fractal* - all. as I say not only omen but amem. about HERE about HAIR as its site & its warlocket

Be careful to be nice to him - this is how 'Bride' begwineth - *because you are not beautiful. Wear enough make-up to let him think you are beautiful but never so much that he knows you are hiding something. . .*

Every one of these poems is one more strand one more curl one more weave of a whole book. recovering back to our culture. from the scalp not *up*. not *down*. not even *across* - all these of course - *yes* - but we into different mathematics now - we into *mathemagicals* - so that the word wd be *roseate* - if you want any word at all

"Pella," you might say again. "There is something I have to tell you..."

Kamau Brathwaite @CowPastor & FlatBush NewYork NewYorl 1 May 2004

CONTENTS

This collection is dedicated to Ivy Adelle Vaughan
(d. September 1992),
Christine Lilyanne Stevenson
(d. August 2000),
and to Brandon Kayin (b. 1997) and Xavi Entale (b. 1999).

With thanks for all that you continue to teach me.

1. HOMES

CHILD OF A LESSER GOD

See Josie.

See Josie watch.

See Josie watch the men.

See Josie watch the men come home.

See her watch them from between two curtains so light she don't even feel them touch her face when she peep.

See her hold her breath so long that when she have to breathe she gasp and swallow.

See her watch the baby-mothers scratch their knee-backs with slippered feet.

See her watch them clutch pastel bundles to bosoms newly stretched.

See her watch them wait for evening child support.

See her hear how Dear Aunt, Mother Maggie, Ms. Raven caught Janiqua, Malaika and Yvonne making the same mistakes they did.

See her hear the grandmas shout to please keep little Andrew and baby Mercedes out of the dew before they catch cold.

See her hear the grandmas groan as they sit stooped in castor-oil-soaked cotton head-ties to chase the cold out of their heads.

See Josie watch the baby-fathers.

See her watch them get off the Friday by-pass with heavy-lidded, home-from-town eyes.

See her watch them slip their fingers into pockets full of minimum wage.

See Josie watch babies and monies pass.

See her watch young mothers laugh at new and easy richness. Hear their deep and mellow voices. See her watch young fathers lift the cotton-weight next generation with hands unaccustomed to fragility. See her watch mothers and grandmothers grudge approval on responsibility, notwith-standing youth, maturity ahead of season, knowledge without age.

★   ★   ★

On a day that demanded the wearing of good clothes (like the first day of any new job), Primus Parris wore his tight, stonewashed jeans, a blue polyester shirt starched and pressed and open almost to his waist, white leather moccasins and the overpowering scent of Right Guard. On this day he also carried a small black plastic bag from which he repeatedly extracted a fine-toothed comb to scrape the drip from his jherri-curls onto the paper towel he had folded neatly along his collar. In another bag, under his right arm, his costume sweated and stank.

Today, Primus Parris was smiling like a little boy with a new wagon at the promise of money. It had been so long since he'd made some and there was nothing like money to remind you you're a man.

The girls in the garden at the church fair tittered as Primus took off his shirt, in broad daylight, and put on his red velvet vest with the gold trimmings. He fitted tassels at his wrists and ankles and a gold paper crown on his head that rang bells every time he moved. He mounted his unicycle, juggling three balls and spinning a wheel on his lower lip.

He loved the applause. But he loved the money more –

the fact that his God-given balance could make him a hundred dollars and a plate of food in a few hours out of one afternoon.

He saw the girl watching him out of the corner of his right eye. She sat beneath the tea tent, untouched white sandwiches oozing pastel fillings on a plate in front of her. Legs demurely crossed at the ankles. He decided to use her for his act. She was the right size. Slightly built.

He dismounted to loud applause.

He whistled to her. She made the usual deflections. It was the same at every show, with every pretty girl he chose from the audience. He confirmed that he really *was* calling her. Made an impatient gesture with his hands. Incited the crowd to spur her on. She demurred. He urged the crowd to clap louder. She surrendered.

He lifted her onto his right shoulder. Felt her thighs tremble when he let her go.

"Steady now," he murmured. "You can grab hold o' me."

She placed a soft hand on the left side of his neck, laced the other into it and stretched her feet out in front of her to steady herself. He mounted the unicycle again. Started a wheel spinning on his left elbow and went riding backwards and forwards across the grass. Giggling girl on the right; spinning wheel on the left; amazed crowd all around. He wondered whether church people were good tippers. Suddenly she tipped off his shoulder, upset the wheel and the cycle and they fell to the grass in one sharp intake of breath. She was alright. Apologizing. The crowd's applause grew thunderous. Sometimes this was the spur they needed to remind them how hard it was. They extracted dollars and cents from pockets and handbags and dropped their appreciations into a red velvet box he had placed there for the purpose. He suspected that later he would find it had been a good take.

Her mother came running. She looked just like her daughter.

She yanked her up by the elbow. Said something about the unseemliness of a young woman being hoisted like a sack of flour on a man's shoulder. He apologized. Neither of them seemed to hear him. The woman took a handkerchief out of her pocket and tried to wipe the grass stains off the girl's skirt. They wouldn't budge. They went to find a standpipe. He mounted the unicycle again. Ever the performer. Break a leg. Show must go on. Head up, keep smiling. Prepare for the finale. Flaming wheels of fire spinning on the edge of his nose. There was a hush with the whoosh of the first wheel. The stunt went well, although he was distracted. Later he tried to explain to himself why he kept looking at those pale white sandwiches from between the rings of flame.

★   ★   ★

She had seen him before, of course.

Last week she had passed the neighbours down the street, reluctantly making her way to Sunday School, though why she should go to any kind of school on Sundays and especially why there should be classes for almost-adults she would never understand. He had been right there in the Handel's front yard, cutting and slicing the silence of Sunday morning with his blue-black arms. Wielding his cutlass with such grace it did not seem that he was moving at all; it looked like he just stood there still and strong and the branches of the sweet-lime hedge just shaved themselves into shape before him. She had passed without a word. You never could tell who was watching. Her mother's hands were quick for talking out of turn. Especially to someone like Primus Parris – who most certainly had nothing and did not even go to church to ask for it.

He had not noticed her then. At least she did not think so.

★   ★   ★

Primus knew he had seen the face before. She was the church girl. She passed him one Sunday he had a job in a yard in Latherby. He had been whistling before he saw her coming. But she was one of those girls you could only observe in silence. And he had.

He had seen her again at her mother's shop. He had gone there one morning, jostling with the wives for a space at the wooden counter. He needed a tube for his unicycle tyre. His fat cousin, with whom he was staying for no other reason than that she was his only connection in this part of the country and flats were hard to come by and harder to keep when you worked the way he did, was in the shop begging the owner for credit. She was pregnant again for an unemployed and unconcerned husband. Primus gave her the odd twenty when his take was good. She acted like he didn't have to but he knew his welcome would wear out more quickly otherwise, and they both knew he planned to stay a while.

The fingers of her ring hand had pinched the counter, deliberately conspicuous in early morning news exchange, to remind all who cared that this was no shame-faced conception (though similarly regrettable). She was entreating Mary Melon to permit her a week's worth of meal provisions until next week when her husband was promised a job. As was her custom she berated him publicly – how was she to manage with another mouth to feed and he not working and Amarice barely cutting her first tooth and the twins just ready to go to school? It was her bad luck to marry a man like the one she had, but could Miss Melon pity her children and give her the credit?

Miss Melon reminded her that the good Lord cared for his own and suggested that maybe if she found herself in church more, she would have less time to make babies in the first place and then, with a rare softness, and momentarily forgetting the rising account, let it drop that she was implementing a new assessment of credit-worthiness from

15

that moment – participation in and attendance at church. Any person who was born again had the blood of Jesus on their heads and could be trusted to repay their debts. And would Mrs. Parris agree to attend the next adult Bible class in exchange for the provisions?

Mrs. Parris hesitated, the eyes of the other women awaiting her reply. The saved among them anticipated another soul won for Christ, while the others merely grumbled their impatience and thought to themselves that, but for the fact that Mary Melon's shop was readily accessible in curlers and a housecoat and was chock-full of forgotten ingredients and a minute away from a simmering pot, they would easily have gone to the supermarket to escape Ms. Melon's preachifying.

Mrs. Parris was not an atheist but neither was she disposed to being shepherded.

Primus said, "I will pay for them."

Those who did not know his origins, and had not realized his connection to Mrs. Parris, observed him with interest.

Miss Melon's eyes turned cold.

"Fix this customer, Josie," she said evenly, and moved on to someone else. And there was the girl again, hands outstretched along the counter, waiting for Mrs. Parris's requests.

Mrs. Parris breathed relief and rattled off a listing to Josie, who gathered everything quickly. Primus added his bicycle tube. Their hands brushed when she tallied their purchases the old-fashioned way – on a page in an exercise book with a pencil that had been sharpened with a knife. $12.21. He placed the money on the counter and her hand slid towards it. He had put down a quarter but he had twenty-one cents. He took back the quarter as she reached for it and their hands brushed again. He put the right change in her open palm. She smiled at him.

When the truth about Josie came out with her belly, the good married women of the community, whose cotton girdles guarded their virtue, felt a guilty gratification. Her mother had rejected the longings of their brothers and uncles (and husbands) – without even a twist of her tongue to show a little "perhaps". Even Mrs. Primus could not help but feel a little redemption. Past kindnesses aside, Mrs. Primus could still call a spade a spade. It had escaped no one that after Mary Melon's first marriage to a preacher had ended when he died in a car accident, she had rejected the postman (who sang tenor in the church and was not known to spend his Friday evenings drinking rum), the organist (whose attention the best spinsters in the congregation had craved at least once in their lives) and even the head server. That the good men of the village were not good enough suggested to the good married women that Miss Melon thought herself too special. That she separated her daughter from theirs and herself from them confirmed it.

The same men that had once leered after Miss Melon's pretty eyes and her smooth J.C. toffee skin, curving tight in all the right places, and then, after she had established her place above them, had crossed the road when they saw her coming, now found her once more sufficiently fallible to free their tongues to call after her. Everyone could understand a parent whose daughter had fallen. It had happened to the best of them.

It was a rainy Lenten Friday. Later, the good married women of the community said that there was little good about it. The young girls had been mouthing hymns with listless eyes under the righteous gazes of good mothers and grandmothers, whose hand-held fans flicked breeze over babies being brought up in religion.

As it is told, Mary Melon left her pew under a big black straw hat with the longest of speckled chicken feathers, suitably sombre in her black gloves, to approach the altar for communion. Here stories diverge. Some say that it was while Miss Melon's back was turned that Josie Melon left the church, a spectre in a frilly white dress more befitting a child than any eighteen-year-old girl, running for dear life the wrong way up the church aisle. Some say that it was after Miss Melon had returned to her seat and had her head bowed in prayer. All agree that at some point during the service Miss Melon recognized that Josie was gone; that she left before the end of the sermon, eyes furtively checking each pew on her way out to try to locate her daughter; that outside, the men on the steps of the rum-shop, to whom Good Friday was nothing but a holiday, whistled and spat their fantasies at her as she fumed her way home; that it was only when she reached her gate and saw her daughter kissing a man, whose feet pedalled back and forth on a unicycle to keep him at her lips, that she realized that there was a peculiar rosiness about her daughter's cheeks, a familiar roundness about her belly that had nothing to do with spiritual rapture.

Some say that Mary Melon rubbed her eyes to test the veracity of her vision and, eyes having told the truth, screamed for blue murder and brought the rest of the congregation running. The good wives of the community confirm that they had had to put Mary Melon to bed, so useless was she to herself on that day. They all agree that she fell asleep with the last of Sister Marshall's convalescence soup and that Sister Irene closed her door and told an anxious Josie in the hall that it was probably better for her to stay in her room and rest, that anxiety was not good for her condition, that Primus should go home and he and Mrs. Parris should come around again in the morning and talk to Mary Melon and make the necessary arrangements.

They all say that when they left the house, both women were peacefully asleep, the doors were unlocked, nothing was lit or burning.

That is why no one could explain the fire.

It was discovered in the wee hours, a paper-boy having seen smoke when he arrived with Miss Melon's *Weekender*. The two bedrooms were charred, the bodies burnt beyond recognition. The rest of the house was virtually untouched.

They were buried side by side in the churchyard to hymns and a rousing sermon about the sting of death and the gift of salvation for the righteous. The house still stands. It is rumoured there are relatives overseas who are to return to sort the affairs. In the interim teenage boys take their conquests there for privacy because younger children and adults avoid it for fear of a spectre they say streaks around in a white frilly dress, looking for something.

See Josie.

See Josie watch.

See Josie watch the men.

See Josie watch the men come home.

See her watch the baby-mothers scratch their knee-backs with slippered feet.

See her watch them clutch pastel bundles to bosoms newly stretched.

See her watch them wait for evening child support.

Hear her singing.

A whispered melody as soft as the wind through a window.

A little song of hope and freedom.

STRANGER IN MY GARDEN

The summer that Chasseyman came was the one that I turned thirteen. Thirteen marked many milestones, some more pleasant than others. Thirteen was the first birthday I bought myself something other than candy and dolls with my birthday money. It was *Every Girl's Garden* by Carol Sanders – which had nothing to do with gardening. It was a book for teenage girls written by a former Miss World finalist. In the prologue she asked me to imagine that each person has a garden in which they cultivate all of the characteristics and qualities (flowers) they need to be happy and successful adults. Then she asked me to think about what flowers girls should have. She thought there were lots – and teenage girls needed to plant them early. Thirteen was the summer I spent reading the book that *Woman's Weekly* found to be "a true gem" and *The Observer* believed to be "a must-read for teenage girls". Thirteen was the last summer my mother came home and the first I left home. And, of course, thirteen was the summer I met Chasseyman.

One day Chasseyman came up the walkway and asked my father if he had any odd jobs he wanted doing. He did. Since my mother first left, my father had no time for our garden any more and it flourished with his inattention and grew over and around itself. Now, he didn't even make half-hearted attempts to tidy it on the weekends before my mother flew in.

Chasseyman was good with the garden. I had never suspected that she was really a woman and when I did find out it was only because one tiny breast fell out of her khaki overalls when she leaned over the gate with a piece of bread for a sparrow. She enjoyed the shock it caused me.

I crashed into the gate on my bicycle, legs straddling the saddle like the wings of a jet, forgetting that I was supposed to apply the brakes. I scrambled away from Chasseyman when she tried to help me. When I ran inside and told my mother (who was at home at the time) that Chasseyman was really a woman, she looked up from her breakfast with a glance reserved for the too-young broaching the unmentionable. Instead of replying to the obvious question, she observed that I had scraped my knee and in the fuss made over finding the cotton wool and gauze, and the sting and protest on the application of alcohol and the band-aid, Chasseyman's true gender was forgotten.

But once freed again to go outdoors, once confronted by the twisted neck of my orange racer, wheel suspended, still spinning, above the okra plants, once reminded of my shock by the smart of my knee, the image of that tiny little breast returned. It was not unlike my own, barely a protrusion beyond the nipple, slightly sagging into view. I wondered if she found hers similarly annoying.

Chasseyman returned to her painting of the garden shed, breasts safely tucked away, whistling a nonsense tune and apparently oblivious to the paint sloshing off her brush and the wall onto her face, her hands and her dirty overalls. Carol Sanders and I sat beneath the breadfruit tree and watched her.

She was not ugly, once examined. She was large – nothing fragile about her – and the red waves of her hair were clipped into a fade more reminiscent of the men in the barber's chair at the market than that of any woman I had ever seen. Underneath the cinnamon fuzz of her eyelashes, the same rusty tone as the rest of her, *her* eyes held no mystery. She could probably have been pretty if you put her in pinks and yellows and darkened her lips. Carol said that red-toned skins were best in those colours – with plum lips – but she just was as she was.

Sadly, many women, not just girls, are victims of the myth that make-up must match wardrobe. This is untrue. Make-up should, first and foremost, match your colouring (hair, eyes, skin) and secondly, complement your outfit. A pink business suit may be beautiful on olive skin, but the overall effect is ruined by pink eyeshadow. A better choice for the olive-complexioned may be an earth-toned or neutral palette.

As a general guide, fair skins are better suited to pinks and corals, medium tones to warmer shades and olive skins to magentas, browns and earth colours.

There are four cardinal rules of make-up for girls:-
1. You should never look like you are wearing any;
2. Never match make-up to clothing;
3. Always test make-up in natural light before buying, and
4. Change products at least every six months.

"Something wrong?" she asked. After jumping out of my skin I re-examined her gravelly voice. Was that what had made me think she was a man?

Moments later I still had not answered her. Eyes closed, face pushed forward into sound, I tried to summon clues. My silence should have puzzled her into repetition and so assisted my cause. But she too fell silent.

And then she touched my arm, as if to rouse me.

"You're a woman," I said, accusingly.

"Last time I checked." She laughed and, pulling her gloves off, wiped the sweat off her brow with her bare fingers.

"That what got you sitting there, staring me down?"

She put her gloves back on. Restarted a song.

"But I saw you," I sputtered, "your breast, I mean. And my mother says no decent woman should be without a bra, even under lots of clothes."

Chasseyman chuckled.

"Well I'm all for you listening to your mother."

And she was back to her garden.

Her laughter riled me, ran roughshod over my pride and rendered it useless. I stomped away.

The day after Chasseyman had finished trimming the hedge, painting the shed and tidying the garden, I was sitting in its new order, dreading the creak of the gate to the verandah. But it gave no warning (Chasseyman having oiled it, I suppose) when my mother appeared before me in the walkway, dressed in her best, lugging her suitcase behind her. She was ready to return. It seemed that every visit started a little later and ended a little earlier than the one before. This one had been just three weeks of summer.

"I am about to leave now, Jane," she said. "Are you going to kiss me?"

I said nothing.

Two vacations ago, when my mother was leaving, I had reacted badly to her attempt to kiss me goodbye. Since then she asked first. I did not want her to ask. I wanted her to kiss me. Hard. As a matter of fact, I wanted her to kiss me so hard she would realize that she did not wish to study in London any more. That she did not want to leave me and my father.

She did not kiss me, not then.

"Now, Jane," she said, rummaging in her purse, "I've explained to you why I am doing this. You *are* sure you understand?"

It was not a real question and she did not repeat it when I failed to answer.

My mother was returning to college. From the argument

she'd had in the den with my father two Januarys before, it was evident she resented having stopped her course to marry him. To have me. He had said, stupidly, "Go ahead, see if I try to stop you." To our surprise, she went ahead. To England, of all places, where she was born and where she was part of a community in which, mentally, I could not place her.

"Jane?"

Sometimes when my mother came back I was so happy to see her that I could not sit still. I would sit beside her in my father's jeep, inhaling the smell of foreign on her clothes, the look of foreign on her skin. I would slide my hands around her waist and snuggle close to her. This would last several days. Until she did something annoying. Something like call me Jane in *that* tone of voice. Something like leave.

"Jane," she reached out to smooth my right eyebrow with a bit of spittle on her finger, "I must go or I will miss my flight."

A taxi pulled up and honked, jolting me out of my annoyance.

"Daddy's not taking you?"

I was indignant without knowing why. I hated going to the airport. Standing in line with her at check-in. Waiting in the departure lounge between the two of them, always silent, listening to travel announcements that were never for me. Watching other people's public partings and dreading my own.

My mother looked back at our house, in which my father lurked invisible. She shifted her weight to the other foot and picked up her suitcase.

"It will save him the trouble… I will miss you, Jane."

She kissed me quickly on my forehead, too quickly for me to move out of the way. Then she was getting in the cab and I was pulling my bicycle from the okra patch and doing it so violently I broke some plants, and I was racing around to the back of the house, willing the wind to wipe my tears.

Every Girl's Garden by Carol Sanders, Chapter 3, page 59

Every young lady needs to learn to control her temper. Who wants to take the trouble to pick a rose that is surrounded by thorns?! Not many, if anybody. It always pays to learn to minimize your prickly bits, so that, even when you are angry or upset, the rose in you still shines through. The pleasant employee, mother, daughter, wife or friend is often the one that brings the best out of other people. A pleasant and even personality helps you when you are in strange situations among people you do not know and will put you, as well as other people, at ease. Here are a few tips I use when in a stressful situation (or anytime I feel I'm about to go 'ballistic'!)

1. Take a deep breath and start counting backwards, slowly, from 10. Don't stop until you feel calmer. Repeat if you speak before you reach 1 or you feel the same way when you get there.
2. Force your voice to remain even when speaking in this state. If you hear yourself getting loud or agitated, stop speaking. Apologize to the person you are speaking to. Go to step one and then start speaking again.
3. Force yourself to smile while speaking in an angry state. It is harder to stay angry with someone at whom you are smiling – and smiles are contagious!!
4. When you are present with other people who are arguing, it helps to offer either or both a glass of water. Then, after your interruption has momentarily distracted them from the argument, ask if there is anything you can do to help them resolve the issue.

My mother and I used to be close.

I could still remember times when I was little and I visited their bedroom at six in the morning and climbed into their bed between them, cocooned in the warm spot they created for me, and spoke to her in soft tones while my father slept. In those times my mother whispered stories about the parts of their lives before I was born and the parts I was too little to remember. She would tell me about a dashing young black medical student who fell in love with a white psychology major. It was the turbulent sixties. They married and had a brown baby and moved back to his little island in the Caribbean where he set up his practice. We both knew that it was our story but she never named names – although I would make her repeat it over and over until she begged me to stop. I realized that if my mother had to tell me that story now, I might have to ask her who the people in the story were.

In those times we would lie still and plan what we would have for breakfast – which somehow always became an elaborate affair. She used to let me break eggs, beat pancake batter and dress everything up with parsley and the tomatoes we cut with a special utensil to make them look like flowers.

We used to tread around the kitchen barefoot and in our nightdresses on those days, and then my father would come downstairs and kiss us both and we would all eat until we couldn't eat any more and then my father and I would go to get the newspaper and when we returned my mother would have cleaned everything up.

In those times it never occurred to me that my mother was anything but happy just being what she was.

After she left for the last time, I re-examined those times for skulking discontent. I rode down the street and with every failure to discover the previously undetected rode that much faster until I was whizzing down the block. I almost collided with Mr. Ginster's old Vauxhall.

The hand that saved me was Chasseyman's.

"You seem hell-bent on hurting yourself with this bike," she observed, staring at me. In her left hand she held a lit cigarette that smouldered and shed ash at our feet. She was ignoring my screeching to be left alone.

"You are such a strange little girl," she exhaled.

"My *name* is Jane," I huffed.

She laughed.

"Well, it certainly doesn't suit you."

On this point I was momentarily silenced by my own concurrence. We stood around – she smoking and me on the saddle of my bike, one foot planted on the ground and the other spinning the pedal the wrong way at increasing speed.

"Madgeline," she said.

"What?"

She was blowing circles with smoke. She was sometimes making lines of them. It was something my mother had recently begun to do. Another one of those things she picked up back in England. Something else she used to do before I knew her.

"If I had to guess, I mean," she continued, "I'd have guessed you a Madgeline. Mysterious women always have names like Madgeline. Jane is so plain – it does you no justice."

I could not decide whether or not she was serious. But I rather liked the concepts of mystery and womanhood. Especially juxtaposed. And I liked the name Madgeline. So I didn't protest.

"Madgie, for short," she ended.

"Yours doesn't sound like you either," I ventured. "What's the real one?"

I remember her laughing, slow and deep. I closed my eyes quickly to see if I would have thought her a man if we were strangers, if I'd just come up the street, new to the neighbourhood, if I hadn't seen that offensive little braless breast.

"Whatever you like."

I had recently become irritated by anything other than direct answers to my questions, asked or un-uttered, so I sucked my teeth at her. She just laughed again and began to walk away.

"Jane!" I shouted spitefully, disrupting the circles of smoke rising over the back of her head and drifting away from me. Carol Sanders was forgotten.

"OK Madge," she answered, "Jane it is. See you around."

Every Girl's Garden by Carol Sanders, Chapter 4, page 104

The swimsuit is the sworn enemy of most women!!! Many a beautiful girl turns to jelly at the prospect of summer and days spent at the beach. But swimwear does not have to strike terror into the heart of any woman, provided that she selects her suit with care and a good eye for what is appropriate for her. What I will say is that it is seldom appropriate or attractive to see a teenage girl in a suit that is not even appropriate for an older woman. String and 'thong' bikinis are best left on the sale rack and rarely complement any shape but a stick-thin model figure. Suits for teenage girls are ideally bright, with appropriate coverage of breasts and behind. With that in mind, the following tips are also useful:-

1. Girls with long, slim legs can wear high-leg swimsuits (not too high!) with bikini cuts but almost any leg-cut will suit them, including boy-cut shorty-shorts, French-cut legs and others;

2. Girls with thicker legs should avoid boy-cuts which make legs look thicker; higher legs give the illusion of leg length and are a better choice;

3. Girls with large bosoms should avoid plunging neck-lines. Stick to demure halter-tops and softly curved designs which flatter chest size and give requisite support;

4. Girls who are plump are better off choosing solid colours or suits with tiny patterns or thin vertical stripes, all of which create the illusion of slimness by drawing the eye lengthwise;

5. For small, boyish bosoms, choose brightly coloured suits or lively brilliant prints with spaghetti straps or none at all, accentuated by shirring or gathering of fabric. Small breasts will be lost in thick-strapped suits in solid dark colours....

My father and I were going to the beach. It was the first Sunday after my mother's last departure and the first time we were venturing out together since the taxi took her away.

When I was little, the beach days were usually Sundays after the big breakfasts. My father and I would come back with the newspapers, he'd give me the comics and my mother the Sunday magazine and we would sit at the newly wiped table and get lost in our bits of the news. When we finished, he would sometimes say, "Go get your trunks, Jane." I would squeal and my mother would smile and I would rush upstairs to find a swimsuit and my mother would come into my room while I dressed and try to tidy my hair while I wriggled into something. My favourite suit was blue with yellow sunflowers all over it. My mother had one just like it that we had bought on a trip to town. Sometimes when we went downstairs my father would say, "I'm the odd man out, isn't there one for me?" and though we knew what was coming we would crack up every time.

We passed the usual coconut stalls, rasta leather-craft carts with the benevolent stare of Haile Selassie emblazoned on everything, people at bus stops dressed for Sunday. I was wearing the blue suit under a towel. It fitted me tightly, the ends of it barely covering the fresh swell of breast and behind. My father wore shorts and a t-shirt. He did not ask if there was a blue suit with flowers for him. We drove with the radio off and the breathless hum of the air-conditioning between us. I remember it being bright outside and people looked happy. I could not hear their happiness – sensing it from the other side of glass.

"Don't roll the window down, Jane," growled my father. "It is too damn hot outside."

I pressed a button and the fresh sliver of sound died. I had spent a long time in their bathroom using his razor to remove my new bikini line and I worried whether I had done a good job.

When we arrived there were boys on the beach.

"Aren't you going in, Jane?" my father asked, sitting on the sand and opening one of his medical journals. *The Medic*, or something like it. "You only have 45 minutes today."

I did not remind him of the obligatory splash he needed to make to get accustomed to the coldness of the water, wetting me in the process and acclimatizing me too.

I walked down the beach, kicking sand into little explosions with my toes. I did not remove my towel.

"Don't go too far," said my father – so I decided that I would.

Then I realized I was calling attention to myself and walked slowly and sometimes circled back in time for his custodial glances, which I timed at about every seven minutes, like contractions.

I saw my mother have them, once. For the baby that died. It would have been a boy. My mother was initially brave; my father devastated. Not because the baby had died but because he had been unable to save it for my mother, who had wanted it desperately. It was soon after we buried it in a little white box at the church, with a teddy bear I had bought it, that my mother decided she was returning to college to finish her psychology degree. My father had said that her healing was one of those things she was unwilling to entrust to anyone but herself – like moving the Waterford crystal to polish the shelf it was on, or whipping the egg whites for her favourite soufflé.

"It is not that she does not love us, Jane," my father had said, "but she must do this on her own."

I sat down to watch a woman bouncing a laughing baby in the foam of dead waves.

"Madgie!"

At first I joined the woman and the baby in looking around for the object of the greeting, but then Chasseyman appeared and I remembered that Madgie was me.

"Oh, hi Jane," I said with sarcasm. Wasted on her.

"This is my friend Angie."

I was so taken with the sight of Angela Marie Hodge that I almost forgot to look for Chasseyman's breasts in her black maillot. (On reflection, barely noticeable. Carol was right about the prints.)

Angie was magazine-pretty. Short and petite but curvy. Skin the colour of roasted almonds. Black hair hugging her scalp in tight curls. Impossibly long eyelashes that shadowed her hazel eyes with the mystery that, despite myself, I was trying to cultivate. Angie knew Carol's secrets already. She wore a high-legged, printed number with spaghetti straps. Her suit became a different colour over her small breasts.

"So have you been in the water?"

"Glorious today!" breathed Angela.

I decided to hate her because she was not only pretty, but good-natured as well. I directed my gaze to Chasseyman.

"I am just sunning today," I said haughtily. "I do not wish to go in the water."

They stared at each other and nodded. Reached for me suddenly and hoisted me by my limbs into the space between them. Carried me, towel abandoned, to the shallow water. Counted to three beneath my screaming and dropped me gasping into weightlessness.

I resurfaced to the sound of my father's voice.

"Jane, are you alright?"

He was, I decided, deservedly worried and I laughed at him. "Fine," I giggled. His doubt was hilarious.

"You are a doctor," I accused him. "Can't you tell whether I am fine or not without having to *ask* me?"

My father looked wounded. He had not recognized that I had the capacity to be so cruel.

Then I started, inexplicably, to cry. They were all silenced by my blubbering. Chasseyman handed me my towel. Angie was apologetic.

"We were just fooling around," she told my father.

"Jane's been having a difficult time," he said.

He offered them a ride home and they accepted. Angie explained that her car was in the shop for the hundredth time this year and she was thinking of changing it. My father started to discuss its symptoms with her. "He thinks he can fix anything which ails," I remember thinking. Chasseyman walked behind with me. Angela and my father walked ahead to retrieve *The Medic* and the keys from under the tree where he had left them.

We rode home in silence.

At nights I had the same dream.

I dreamt that my mother, my father, Angie and Chasseyman were in a room talking in low voices. I was outside the door in my blue bathing suit with my brother. In my dream he was five, but I knew it was him. Cute and harmless. He whispered to me like a co-conspirator, knowing we should not be eavesdropping. The flowers on my swimsuit grew three-dimensional and started to fall off, one by one, which my brother seemed to find fascinating. Soon we were no longer listening to what the adults were saying. Three flowers remained – two covering my breasts and one between my legs. My brother started to disappear in pieces until just his pointing hand was left, stuck in a permanent gesture of amazement at my suit. I was so scared I decided to run inside the room to my parents and my mother caught sight of me on the threshold.

"Jane," she said reprovingly, "go back outside."

"But Mum," I always said, "can't you see the flowers?"

Angie came to the house one lazy, lonely day when my father was busy in his clinic and I was lying in the garden watching Chasseyman prune bougainvillea and reading snippets of Carol Sanders. She arrived in a little yellow VW Beetle.

Even her car was pretty. And she handled it with grace and confidence. She told us that she came to apologize for upsetting me at the beach, but after this she was still hanging around and she finally asked for my father.

We directed her to the clinic.

Chasseyman started cutting the saplings too far away from their knots.

"You said they'd die if you cut them that way," I reminded her.

Her song stopped and she sucked her teeth instead.

"Carol Sanders says sucking your teeth is unladylike," I said.

"I've never pretended to be a lady," replied Chasseyman.

But she stopped to light a cigarette and observe the house when she thought I wasn't looking. We watched them come outside together. My father walked Angie to the Beetle, which she got into and coaxed to life. They laughed. He seemed to be apologizing for having to rush back to his patients, but we were far away so maybe he wasn't.

After Angie left he waved at us and returned to his clinic.

"Let sleeping dogs lie," muttered Chasseyman. She swatted a bug that had trapped itself in the sweat coating her bare leg.

"Does Angie want my father?" I asked.

"How should I know, Madgie!" exclaimed Chasseyman, but her voice was unsteady.

"Well, does she usually want a lot of men?"

"A lot of men usually want her," Chasseyman replied.

When I saw Angie again a week later it was because my father stopped by the house on the way to a date with her. She sat in the front seat of the Land Rover, smiling and self-assured while my father explained to Chasseyman that he would be late, ensured she had his mobile and his pager numbers and told her to make herself at home. It was the first time I detected any animosity between Angie, who stayed in the car, and Chasseyman, who stayed on the verandah with me. They did not speak to each other.

"How long have you known her?" I asked Chasseyman later when, past my bedtime, we were snuggled on the sofa, watching comedy re-runs.

"We go way back," she said. She was one of those people who laughed hard at the funny parts in comedies, even the ones you knew were coming, that a blind man could see a mile off.

"How did you meet?" I insisted.

"*Ha. Ha. Ha.* At college. We did a class together. *Hahaha.* She was the girl that all the girls hated and the boys couldn't get enough of and she didn't care either way. *Hehehe. Madge, did you see that?*"

I knew the girl she was talking about. There was one in my class. A girl whose burgeoning breasts, which she freely displayed and carried with confidence, were big news to everyone but herself. The rest of us hid ours as best we could.

It transpired that Chasseyman had studied art at college. She was pretty good, too, but she wasn't crazy about teaching, so she mostly travelled from country to country and did odd jobs and painted and sculpted and crafted and drew. She planned to mount an exhibition when she finally returned to America. She was going to call it "Travelling Band", though she wasn't really sure why. The name just came to her in a dream like her pieces often did.

But I wanted to get back to the point.

"Did you like her from the first time you saw her?"

"Certainly did," said Chasseyman and she stopped laughing at the movie. Several jokes passed in silence.

It might have been something about the way she said "certainly" with the colours of the TV flashing her face in every shade of green and blue. It might have been the way her face lit up and then clouded back over. It might have been nothing at all. But something about that moment reminded me of the way my father had said, "It is not that she does not love us, Jane… but this is something she must do on her own."

"Chasseyman," I said, "Did you love her?"

And studio audience laughter punctuated the silence in the moments before she said, "Yes, Madgie, I really did."

Every Girl's Garden by Carol Sanders, Chapter 6, page 167
Dating is appropriate for a teenage girl of the right age and mental and emotional maturity. Parents are a good gauge of when this time has arrived since it has nothing to do with age and varies from person to person. Parents are also very good assessors of the characters of young men, who should always be introduced to your family first before any dates that are not in crowds of more than four people and at public affairs or events. First dates should always take place at public events with appropriate chaperones. It is perfectly acceptable for a girl's mother to chaperone her daughter and a date to a movie. Dates are not good reasons to forget one of the cardinal rules of make-up – for teenage girls, less is always more…

My first date was with Angus McNichols. It was not an official date. The big-breasted girl was having a party and invited us both, and Angus came up to me after biology and said, "You going to the party?" as if there was only one party worth his mention and I said, "Yeah," in what I hoped was my most nonchalant tone, and then he said, "Well, I'll see you there and I'm gonna dance with you all night." And he stared at me with his deep black eyes before walking off. By any account, Angus was bad news – disruptive in class, never in full or prescribed school uniform, promoted each year by the skin of his teeth. Angus was also the best cricket player in his age group, a truly beautiful fourteen-year-old and the object of the affections of every girl in my year.

And he had chosen me.

On the night of the party my father was out with Angie and I was a mess. Chasseyman stood behind me in my bedroom, watching me apply a thick layer of lip gloss in accordance with Carol's colour scale, which lay open on my dresser.

"You don't need any make-up, Madgie," she said. "You are already a beautiful girl."

"That's not the point," I fumed. I could not get the lining right with my unsteady, unpractised hand. I had drawn myself a pair of ridiculous clown-lips that bordered my own by miles.

Chasseyman laughed.

"Well, I have to take you and have you back by eleven," she said, "and it is already nine."

She shook her keys for emphasis. I erased my lips with a balled-up tissue and started again, with the same effect.

"Carol Sanders does not know what she's talking about," I fumed at Chasseyman.

"Perhaps it worked for her," said Chasseyman.

When we arrived at the party it was almost ten. Chasseyman said she would not leave since she would have to return in an hour. But she would not embarrass me by coming inside. She would wait outside in the car.

I had worn jeans and a pink shirt that belonged to my father, rolling up the sleeves and bagging the waist at the top of my jeans as was fashionable at the time. Once inside I presented the birthday girl's mother with her gift and wandered around aimlessly with the aim of finding Angus.

I saw him in a dark corner. With the birthday girl. I stood in the shadows with another girl from my class, whom I imagine Carol would have described as "thick-set" and for whom she would surely have prescribed dark solid colours and modest leg styles. The girl had a bad case of acne, a permanent giggle and black nail polish and was giggling over her punch as we watched them.

"Angus is so coooool," she gushed.

"He's alright." I said, as if I did not care. But I watched him like a hawk.

"Marcia told me that he asked Helena to be his steady tonight." She spoke through five fingers covering her mouth – as if trying to stem the betrayal of a confidence. "But don't tell anybody I told you." She was giggling again.

There was something caught in my chest that was threatening to burst. Angus would never be mine, our love derailed before it even got on track by a train of the big-breasted variety.

They were playing a slow song.

"I didn't think Helena was his type," I said acidly.

The girl almost dropped her punch.

"Are you kidding!!!!!!" she exclaimed. "Every boy in the school likes Helena. Angus cut the cake with her tonight. Petra told me that he went into the bathroom and brushed his teeth with a toothbrush he had brought just in case she asked him. Can you imagine?!!! Mr Super-Cool Angus??" She was talking through her fingers again, "But don't tell anybody I told you."

Helena was wearing a deep pink lipstick that should not have complemented her olive skin, but did. She was in a short pink skirt, the precise shade of her lips, and her big breasts were jiggling in a loud paisley-print shirt with a plunging neckline.

"Where does her mother get her clothes? A strip-club?"

"Oh no," says Giggles, as if it were the most natural question in the world, "Helena buys all her clothes herself in town. Sonia said that she has her own credit card." She looked at me with the now familiar expression of apprehension. "But don't tell anyone I told you."

We watched Helena and Angus dance one song after another. Eventually Giggles got tired and wandered off to the gossip at the drinks table. I stayed in place watching the couple from the dark, like a ghost.

Which is why I did not see Chasseyman until she was right next to me.

"Madgie, it is after eleven. We have to leave," she said, reaching for my arm.

I twisted myself away from her. "I'm not ready," I said coldly.

Chasseyman's brown eyebrows raised perceptibly.

"Well, we have to go, you have no choice."

She reached for my arm again and again I twisted away.

"Leave me alone!" I said, too loudly.

Angus's eyes turned away from Helena's breasts at the sound of my voice, just in time to see Chasseyman lift me off my feet under her arm, and start to take me outside, kicking and screaming.

"Put me down!" I was yelling. "I'll tell my father! You have no right to treat me like a child!"

Chasseyman did not set me on my feet until we were outside Helena's front door, standing among the potted palms in her verandah.

"No. *I* will tell your father," she said. "If you insist on behaving like a child, then I have no choice but to treat you like one!"

Her voice was loud too.

Helena and Angus and a few of their friends were looking openly at us. I imagined Giggles saying, "I hear that her mother left them – but don't tell anyone I told you." The music stopped. The lights came on. Helena's mother started to sparkle under the new lights in a gold dress, gold lipstick and gold shoes. She was at least 300 pounds but she did not look like the sort of person that would tolerate Carol Sanders telling her about it.

"Is everything alright?" she asked.

"Jane is past her curfew and does not want to go home," Chasseyman explained.

"Jane is past her bed-time," sing-songed a voice from the

crowd, which made a collective snigger. Angus was laughing with his arm around Helena's waist.

"Oh, it's alright, Jane," started Helena's mother but I did not hear her since I was stomping off to the car, all the while wondering why I could not stop myself from doing so, why I could not rewind my life back to an hour before, why I could not rewind it to the beginning of the summer, before my mother left, or to the time before she first went back to college.

Later, as I cried in the silence of the car as Chasseyman drove me home, I wondered why I could not find a single thing to say to her.

Every Girl's Garden by Carol Sanders, Chapter 3, page 63
The ability to apologize for wrong actions, to acknowledge and correct improprieties, is a commendable character trait which every person should develop, women especially, as the natural peace-makers of the species. It is also one of the hardest things any human has to learn to do as it goes against the inborn egotistical urge to be right. This is, moreover, why the ability to apologize for misdeeds, once cultivated, is the hallmark of a strong and grounded character...

"I'm sorry."

We were retiring my bike from active duty. In silence. There had been few words between us since the Angus Episode, which is how I referred to the night of the party.

"For what?" grunted Chasseyman. It was not that she was so simple that she did not know what I was referring to. She was testing my sincerity by making me spell it out.

"For being such an idiot at the party the other night." I don't know why my voice broke on the last words, but it did.

So did Chasseyman's.

"I was just trying to get you home when your Dad said you had to be home, Madgie."

It was a comfort to me that she was still calling me "Madgie". Like a confirmation of something unspoken.

"I know. Thanks."

The frame of my bike had twisted in my last escapade and I had decided that it was getting too small for me anyway. We had decided – before the Angus Episode – that we would dismantle it and use the parts in the garden. We would make a sculpture from the wheels, let the rubber tires hold plants, spray-paint the handlebars gold and bend the spokes into interesting shapes. That was Chasseyman's job.

The postman came and my father had to come out of his clinic to sign for a letter, which annoyed him so much that he did not stop to wave at us before returning inside. But then he shouted, "Jane!" Chasseyman said to go ahead, she would wait until I returned to finish up.

I remember thinking that the coolness of the examination room was a marked contrast to the heat outside. Into it my father piped polite jazz tunes. The chairs for patients were antique mahogany; there were paintings and plants, a polished wooden floor. I had really not been in that room on many occasions before. In his chair, in his white coat, behind an imposing polished wooden desk, I saw my father as the awesome person some of his patients saw, and I was a little afraid of him. I wondered what he was like when he gave people bad news about parts that were not working properly, unsuccessful remedies, days left to live. I suddenly realized that in here he was nothing like the man who made one half of the cocoon I used to snuggle into on Sunday mornings. As I entered he removed his stethoscope from his neck and placed it on his desk.

"Jane," he said, "your mother will finish her course this month. But she will stay on. She wants you to go to her."

He did not seem perturbed. He was reflective, as if deciding on a new course of treatment for a non-responsive ailment.

"Why?" I asked. Stupidly, because I knew.

"Jane, your mother is not coming back home."

It was quiet. The rooms were sound-proofed, to give patients privacy, I suppose. Nobody wants the world to hear them fall apart. I could not speak at first, but I did not want to cry. It was as if a sick relative I had long been grieving for, through several stages of deteriorating health, had finally died. I felt a guilty relief.

"Why?" I asked again.

He looked as if he wanted to tell me, but he took in my pink t-shirt with the yellow sequins, my yellow capri pants and my sea-green sandals and I watched him stop himself.

"One day you will understand," he replied. "I don't want you to see this as a choice, Jane. You will still have both your parents – just in different places, that's all."

"I will not," I replied angrily. It was more my anger which prompted tears than any sorrow at the end of their marriage as I knew it. I heard Carol telling me to count backwards from ten. I ignored her.

"True," my father said, giving the wrong answer, "but it will mean less to you in time."

This time I took Carol's advice and smiled at him. Just as she predicted, he smiled back. But he seemed bewildered. As if the symptoms of a new illness had confounded him.

But I was still angry.

"Why are you doing this?" I heard myself screeching, "Why are you doing this to me?"

"Jane," he said, "we would never do anything intentionally to hurt you. It is just that – well… I suppose your mother and I are not in love any more the way you need to be to stay married…"

"That's a load of shit!" I said.

His face tightened. He had never heard me swear before.

"Now, Jane," he said loudly, "I will not tolerate your swearing at me – under *any circumstances!*"

41

"Would you like a glass of water?" I asked him, from somewhere in chapter 3. In my mind I was saying "I am bringing out the rose in me, I am bringing out the rose in me, Iambringingouttheroseinme, Iambringingouttheroseinme. . ."

His perplexity was open and undoctorly.

"No," he answered. "Do you?"

"No," I said.

We said nothing for a while. It did not seem appropriate to go and cry on his lap, although that was what I wanted to do. I felt like one of those children who sometimes wander off and get lost in the mall and are found only after the security guard has required the parents of "Angie" in a red shirt and blue skirt with black hair or "Dickie", who says his mother's name is Elaine, to pick them up at the information desk.

"I am sorry you have to go through this, Jane," he said. But he did not seem sorry that he was going through it himself.

"Would you like me to talk to her for you?" I offered.

"No thanks," he said, smiling. He stood up and ruffled my hair. Put his stethoscope back around his neck. Doctor again.

"OK," I said, and I left.

When I returned outside it was as if our conversation had never happened. I smiled brightly at Chasseyman while defiantly rubbing away the tears from my cheeks and we returned to our garden. In silence again. But this time we both knew it had nothing to do with each other.

The day that Chasseyman left was a week before my own departure. My father had her over to dinner at our house and loudly exaggerated her contribution to the up-keep of our garden. Our conversation was stilted and I insisted on drinking two glasses of wine, which my father allowed. At seven he ate the last of his dessert and got up to leave. He had another date with Angie, who sent her regards and best wishes to Chasseyman via my father, who dutifully recited them over the salmon.

Chasseyman had an early morning flight. My father had agreed to take her to the airport, so she was going to stay with me while he went out and then sleep over. We both had grown to hate goodbyes so we agreed that I would not get up the following morning for the ride to the airport. We would say our goodbyes when my father left.

For dinner I had painstakingly applied lipstick and eyeshadow. I had dressed in a pair of earrings my mother had left, a pair of her high heels, several strands of her pearls and a blue silk shirt my aunt had sent her from Paris, which I paired with my own denim jeans. In the end I looked nothing like her at all.

After my father left to pick up Angie, Chasseyman and I sat in our new garden space, beside the bicycle monument.

"What are we going to do to remember this summer?" she asked me.

"I thought we would just try our best to forget it," I said.

Chasseyman laughed.

"We could bury stuff," she said.

"*Bury* stuff?"

"It's always a good way to deal with things you want to forget," said Chasseyman.

We went among her suitcases to find something she could bury. At some point when I wasn't with her she must have packed and put them at the bottom of the stairs by the door. She decided on a picture of her that she had always hated. She had weighed almost 200 pounds then and she was wearing a swimsuit with a frill around the waist – the kind they make to flatter fat people, the kind that Carol would have approved of. I told her that she had looked like Miss Piggy in a tutu and she said thanks. I decided to bury Carol Sanders. I was not aggrieved by my decision. I was finding it hard to get past chapter 4.

We dug a hole by flashlight and put our things inside. Before we closed it up she asked if there was anything else.

There was. I went upstairs and returned with the blue swimsuit and deposited it in the hole. She looked at me like she wondered if I was sure. I was. We covered the hole with a bicycle wheel that Chasseyman had bent. She had broken the spokes and curled them upwards like so many strands of curly hair. She had painted the whole thing gold and interwoven the circumference with bits of straw and vine and dried foliage.

"So are you looking forward to London?" she asked, after we returned inside to watch more comedies.

"No," I answered.

"It's a great place if busy is what you like," she offered.

"I don't," I said. Suddenly I was sad.

"I didn't either," she said, and we both burst out laughing.

"Is that supposed to cheer me up?"

"Just telling you, that's all."

And then I started to cry.

"They are such children!" I sobbed.

Chasseyman nodded, knowing better than to acknowledge my tears.

"It's the hardest thing about being an adult, you know," she said, "being a child too."

When my father returned from his date it was after midnight and I remember watching him come through the front door, absentmindedly feeling in his pocket for something. I had fallen asleep on Chasseyman's lap in front of the TV. My father lifted me up to take me to bed. I wondered if he could see that I had grown breasts and if so, what he thought of them. He had never acknowledged that they were there.

"Wait," I remember saying to her through sleep, "what's your *real* name?"

"Portia," said Chasseyman, "but don't tell anybody!"

I named my first daughter after her.

THE ILLUSION OF RAIMENT

To see him from a distance you could not say that he deserved this. To look at his half-nakedness from the broken back door with the wind whipping your face and your eyes squinting under the shadow of your hand, you would not think him appreciably flawed. Your stomach would not churn at the smell of him because you would be far away and perceive him only with your more distant senses – your eyes and maybe your ears if he is scolding the cows for straying or singing to the sheep – even though he cannot sing. Your intimate senses would not register the calluses on his hands when he touches you or the rawness of his unwashed smell or the taste of the mud living under his nails when he reaches up to remove a smudge off something that you meant to eat. Not from a distance.

If you start to walk towards him you might quietly lament how, absently, he reaches into the back of his pants and scratches the crack of his ass. Or how he treads barefoot on sheep dung and nettles and stinging ants. You also might feel again, like the reflux of acid from your stomach, the grate of the thick skin on the soles of his feet when they rub against you in bed. He does not need shoes. When he plucks a tick off a cow, squashes it between his fingers and wipes the blood on his pants you might feel yourself recoil.

You might stop then and pull some running vine from the carrot bed you tried to make – which never bore carrots – and the vines might cut your fingers and refuse to budge and you might curse and swear that these vines will be the death of you – just to have a little something to do with your hands. Just to delay the evidence of his imperfections when you get closer. Just to have a little more play at not being disturbed by his commonness. Before you tell him.

On your knees in the carrot bed, after covering them with your skirt because the earth chafes your skin terribly, although Pella's is immune to it, you might think it was always this way. That you always stomached this quiet loathing for the love of your life. That you always knew him to be ordinary and brutish and lacking the fine threads of cultured living. But a fistful of ravaged vines later you might concede that it was not always this way. You might remember yourself then, innocent, just as he still sees you. No learning that was not by trial and error, no secrets, no sins. You might remember yourself then as naïve – or was it just uncomplicated? As you start to approach your husband in the field, you might wonder which one you really were.

Your feet safe from the bare earth within new, store-bright shoes, your head from the hot sun, your eyes from the glare and your hands from the grass, you remember the morning of your first day at university when Ma Wells made dumplings and sardine stew and sliced a store-bought cake and Pella had his old Ford truck warming up outside, still wheezing and catching breath from when it coughed to a start eight minutes earlier. You recall that you minced around in too-big jeans that Pella bought for you, that his sister said he had never bought anything for her, and after all she was his sister. You remember the guilt you felt for going to pursue full-time schooling instead of helping Pella on the farm but he himself had told you to go ahead, he would manage and he wanted you to do whatever it was that made you happy. Secretly you thought that he might actually have been a little relieved to get rid of you for a few hours each day because you were not doing so well on the farm, though you wanted so badly to, and Ma Wells was grumbling and telling you not to bother, that she would do this and she would do that because she would have to do it over anyway when you thought you had finished. You remember wishing that your mother had been there that morning because she could see that you were finally off to get the learning that she swore would elude you for marrying beneath you.

You made light of the cake but the dumplings were too hard, though you really tried lest Ma Wells misinterpret your difficulties as having their origins in your breeding. But when Pella said, "Come on it's time to go", there were many still on your plate and Ma Wells was looking at them and beginning to swell. She wondered aloud whether that was all you intended to eat and whether people did not believe in big breakfasts where you were from, as if it was a foreign place and not the same country. She had started to shake her bangles and the children looked up from the rocks they were lining up on the floor because they knew what her bangles meant and you did not. Pella had said "Ma…" as if he was warning her and you remember that you had not wanted them to get into another fight because of you, so you forced the dumplings in at speed and no sooner had they gone down than they came back up again and you had to change your jeans and Ma Wells went off to her room and left Pella to clean it all up because she said she didn't want it said that she had force-fed anybody and killed them, and Pella's sister returned to the pot for the remainder of your portion because she said that she couldn't stand to see uppity people let good food go to waste.

You remember how tightly Pella held your hand all the way to the door of the first class, even when he was driving, and how he told you that you would be just fine and he loved you and you were the best thing in his life and perhaps the sickness meant a baby – and he had looked so rapturous when he said it that you almost wished it yourself, for him. But when the Ford went trembling back down the hill you remember thinking that you had to be sure there would be no babies, at least until your studies were finished and something had been made of your life. Love Pella though you did, you would not tell him because you knew that babies were a priority for him, although his sister already had so many.

At fifty yards, when he turns around and is beginning to smile because he sees you coming, his wife whom after four years he thinks he loves more than he did when you first met, you try to figure out when it all changed. You admit that it could have started the day you noticed Andra. Andra, the genius of your "Law in Society" class. The man who sat two rows in front of you to the left and knew all the right answers and all the ideology behind what made the headlines in the newspapers that Pella only bought on Sundays to check the prices of vegetables. You remember, with a smile, the multisyllabled words that slid from Andra's lips because they sent you home to your Oxford 2nd ed., and every time you found the meaning of something else it sent a thrill down your spine. But to attribute the beginning to that event leaves too much of the responsibility with you. So you conjecture that perhaps it might have been the night when Pella collected you both from the library and offered Andra a piglet he said had just been weaned and would be ready for Christmas. Pella thought it natural that every man would want to grow the food he fed himself and his family and you were embarrassed because Pella did not understand that

Andra is one of those people who only appreciates a pig after it has already become ham.

"A pig?" Andra had laughed. "Where on earth would I put it?" And you think that perhaps it could have started at the precise moment that you did not say, "A pen."

Though it might have been the following day when Andra told you to let Pella know that his car was out of the shop and he would drop you home now and Pella need not worry, you would be safe with him and you were flattered that he would offer, so you said yes even though he had already tried to kiss you and you could not understand why you, a happily married woman, liked the thought so much. But you told yourself that you were playing a part in reconciling mother and son since Pella would be free again to collect Ma Wells from Mothers' Union meetings and Church Brigade and mid-week services.

You assume that it developed on those Wednesday nights when there was no need to rush because Pella would be home late and so would Ma Wells, and Andra took you out for drinks after your late night class to a place you had never been before with soft lighting and jazz and people who knew him and joined your table and talked about the news just like Andra did. Eventually you talked the same way and on Wednesdays, when Andra dropped you home, it always felt like waking from a dream. You used to go inside reluctantly and change into your nightgown and, if you were careful, look so much like you'd been there for a while that you sometimes even convinced yourself that you had and time spent with Andra had indeed been a dream.

But now, twenty-five yards from your husband, who is opening his mouth and chasing the cows back because he knows how nervous you feel around them, now you conjecture that even if you cannot put your finger precisely on when it started, you know the moment when its existence became firmly entrenched. When you could not deny it even if you wished to. It was the first Wednesday that Andra had suggested coming back to his apartment after class instead of going to the library as you usually did. It was the moment you crossed the threshold of his doorway and let him sit you down on his couch and pour you a glass of wine and fetch you a newspaper. It was the hour he started to make you a dinner of stuffed bell peppers with Mexican rice, the minutes he sat and ate with you, the second he cleared the table and led you to his room without your objection.

You were surprised at how little you thought of betrayal in the lead-up. How even when Andra's breath was in your hair, his lips on your neck, his hand on your cheek, his thighs against your own, all seemed separate and distinct from Andra. All that consumed you was that moment. That disrobing when you stood naked and confessed that it was precisely where you wanted to be and that was all that mattered.

Now, almost up to Pella, you might concede that it might not matter when it all changed. When you first noticed that Andra's sighs when he is sleeping are as measured as his speech. When you last smelled fertilizer in the air when Pella crawled into bed beside you. When it occurred to you that Andra could spell adultery and Pella, in all probability, could not. And it mattered.

And when you reach him you know he does not realize that the sky is falling down. From this proximity the wind is rustling your hair and threatening to cast off your hat, flushing your face, shifting your collar to look for your bra, lifting the edge of your dress and showing your smooth, smooth legs.

From this close, Pella might think you perfect. He might think to himself for the thousandth time how beautiful you are, how ladylike, how lucky he is that you are his own. He might look at you and not see it. He might smile and his generous lips split in a gap-toothed welcome and his tongue might stumble as he calls your name and it may only be the fact that you do not answer him, suddenly cannot look him in the eye, that may make him lose his smile, his composure and his unapologetic innocence, and whereas when he caught sight of you he was sure of all the things he was going to say – the trivial bits about the price he got for the cows he sold today or the progress of the sick lamb he told you about or his negotiations with a new supermarket – now he might not try to say anything. Now he might find himself stripped of the words you are suddenly swathed in.

"Pella," you might begin, because it is 11:45 and Andra had said "12 noon", as they did in the Westerns you both enjoyed so much and he'd also said that if you were not at the gate he would assume that you had changed your mind and he would proceed to the airport alone because he intended to be in Cayman Islands by tomorrow to start his new job in off-shore banking, and you know you must do the necessary before you hear his car horn because the one thing you are sure of is that you are going with him. He has promised you jazz and sunsets and stimulating conversation and art. But Pella deserves some sort of explanation, even though you are not sure exactly how you will explain it to him when you cannot do so to yourself but you believe you owe him that much.

'Pella,' you might say, 'There is something I have to tell you.'

WARRESS

The lizards told my Nanan – to hear her tell it – one, on Route 18, on the way to Sunday-go-to-meeting, the second, just as frisky as can be, landing on her lap in the middle of Mourning Ground. Then a green grasshopper tried its best to settle on my mother's head at the kitchen table and she tried to dodge it and eat her sardine stew without choking, until Nanan just threw her fork right at the top of my mother's head and speared the grasshopper through the middle onto the partition where he died frozen, dripping green. My Nanan knew then. But my mother just stared at that grasshopper and started to be sick in the middle of wailing, and that time it wasn't on account of morning sickness.

My Nanan says she did not put my mother out at the door because the ancestors told her who I was, so she waited for me first and then she did not put my mother out because when I came she was so happy to see me she could not be bothered where my mother was. She didn't tell my mother either that she read the pebbles and knew who my father was – she acted like it was her ex-boyfriend and saved my mother the explanation. My Nanan says that it did not matter who my father was. The ancestors would have chosen anyone, just so I could be born. My Nanan says that I would have been born without one.

My Nanan says it thundered and lightened terrible when I was coming, and the chickens kept running inside they were so terrified and my mother was scared too, so she kept screaming and my Nanan says she told her to be quiet and stop unsettling things, because my mother's screaming kept making the lantern shiver, threatening to extinguish the flame my Nanan was staring at through the glass, so the ancestors could lead her through the spell she needed to say for me to be born the right way. My Nanan says that no matter what anybody says, she knew I was special and she couldn't have my mother upsetting me before I even came out, 'cause then I might have decided not to bother and then the ancestors would have had to wait another hundred years until the stars lined up just right for another me to be born. And who wants to wait that long for the same thing to happen, just 'cause somebody messed up the first time? My Nanan says it is very important for women like me to be born in absolute quiet.

When I finally decided to come out, after the lightning and the thunder had stopped, and it was just a light rain falling (a special rain, my Nanan says, one that falls in one place and not in others and you can step in it and right back out if you want to), I was covered in the caul that marks us and my Nanan says that then she knew for sure (not that she doubted herself in the first place). My Nanan says she took me out and wrapped me up in a blanket she had made special for me and gave me to my mother and took all the stuff that came out with me outside and buried it, 'cause my Nanan says it is important that nobody knows where our stuff is buried. It is like a weakness. My Nanan says my mother cursed and said she was a damn crazy woman, but my Nanan says she went anyway because she knew.

So here I am – Ann. Short for Anointed.

"Keep a new mother indoors for nine days after delivery, with the doors and windows closed to prevent lining cold and cover all her orifices and bind her stomach tight…"

Soon after that my mother left our house at the side of the river and went to America to be a star. I guess America is closer to the sky. I remember her taking me to the embassy with her to get a visa. The thing about women like me is that we remember everything, even stuff that happened before we were born so I don't know why my mother is surprised when I tell her stuff she did when she was little. My Nanan is never surprised. She just tells me not to tell everybody.

Anyway, one day my mother took me to the embassy with her and we stood outside in a long line in the sun with hundreds of people and we waited. When we went inside a man with a moustache questioned my mother about why she wanted to go to America. My mother said her auntie was very sick and she needed to take care of her. And the man said, "How do I know you will come back?" My mother said she was leaving her baby here and that is how I knew I would not be going with her. There was a woman crying at the next window and she stopped me from hearing what else my mother had to say. "Please," the woman at the next window was saying, "I only want to do a little shopping." But I knew she was lying. I recognized her. She had come to my Nanan's window the night before for a spell for good luck and my Nanan had given her for free because she saw that the woman just wanted a chance to work and help out her family. Her tears did not move the woman behind the desk and she stamped her passport refused.

Outside the woman was cursing my grandmother and my mother when she came out to go to the collection window. She said we were a bunch of crazy, loony women who sold bad spells and tricked innocent people out of their hard-earned money. My mother said she had never sold a spell in her life and she had better shut her mouth or she would slap her into tomorrow. The woman came to test her but somebody pulled her away and my mother went to collect her passport.

I asked my mother why she didn't say that she wanted to go to America to be a star and she heard me but she knew that I was a baby and babies are only supposed to gurgle at that age, so she ignored me. My Nanan said that is why my mother cannot be one of us – because she doubts the things she already knows, which is a thing worse than murder and surer in its destruction than death. My mother was just so happy to get her visa that she kissed me quiet and went to collect her passport.

She did not tell my Nanan she was going. The wind told Nanan that, late though it was. To hear Nanan tell it, there she was in the pasture beating her whites on the rocks and the wind whispered something foul and, just so, she dropped her clothes and spoiled my diapers for a week, and she was running. But by the time she got to the house the bedroom was empty save for me in my crib, watching her. My Nanan said I did not even cry. I was already stronger than she was, cause she cried like a baby.

"For an inattentive lover use two drops of rose oil and one of the sap of love grass slow-cooked over a red candle with three strands of your lover's hair and a special prayer. For an inattentive parent there is no cure."

At first my Nanan thought of taking me to my mother and leaving me there, but she says that the ancestors told her everything was as it should be. There would be no chance of my mother poisoning me with her doubts if she was far away. So we store the barrels we get from heaven behind the chicken coop. With time they soften and crumble and the brown paper comes off in layers. Inside them, I play house, I play school, I play doctor. But chickens cannot always do the things you want them to do in those games and there are no other children who can come to play with me. My Nanan says they want to, but their mothers and fathers won't let them on account of how special I am. My Nanan says some parents are afraid of special, especially when it is in somebody else's children, so I mostly play alone. The barrels disintegrate until they are just two rings of metal at either end with some paper in between and some bleeding letters. They cannot stand the wind and the rain and the sun and the bottoms of my shoes and the feel of my strap when we play school. They are just like my mother.

My Nanan unpacks La Chin egg noodles and the New Improved Lemon-Scented Tide and starch you spray from a can and don't have to mix yourself and meat in cans and orange cheese we sniff with suspicion. There are shiny black shoes for me (too small) and yellow frilly dresses (too big) and red panties with rows and rows of white lace on the back (just right). There are hats for Nanan that she stores beneath her bed, and money.

"Continued poverty means either a failure to acknowledge the ancestors and thank them for their help or the spell of a malevolent friend. For both, the remedy is the libation for prosperity, the building of an altar to the ancestors – and the careful avoidance of sweeping the feet during house-cleaning (it delays the trapping of a good husband and is a recipe for sure starvation)."

My Nanan sees her client at the window to our bedroom when I am safe in bed, beneath the quilts she has made from old wedding dresses, christening gowns – clothes for special occasions and deaths. "Not yet," she says, when I protest to come with her. "You have not yet learnt everything and the very people who coo how beautiful you are when they need our help will tear out your eyes in the street if something goes wrong." The image of somebody tearing out my eyes keeps me out of sight when people come. For most, she just reads the pebbles or a special bowl of water they have stirred with their left hand. For others she goes into her wardrobe and extracts a grass or a leaf or a root to boil or burn or bury, which she wraps in brown paper. For emergencies – like a person on their death-bed or a fight where too much blood has been spilt – she removes her warmth and her many petticoats and drags on a dress made spring-fresh in the new washing machine and hurries out after waking up an ancestor to look over me. Sometimes, if she will be long, she will take me with her and put me in another room to rest until she is finished. At these times I cannot sleep. I think that I am in the house of the very people who will tear my eyes out and I do my best to avoid looking at them. Which is often the same as they do to me, so it's just as well. Once, my Nanan went to help this woman whose belly was big with a new baby. When we went through the door I saw the baby's spirit trying to decide whether to stay or to leave. The woman was bleeding and my Nanan sent her other child into another bedroom with me. We stared at each other for the longest while. She was looking at my long hair, which my Nanan usually keeps covered in the daytime so people cannot see my power. She was looking at my long purple dress and my petticoats and my amulets and my armbands and she said, "My mummy said your granny is a witch." And I said, "She is not. We are medicine women and for generations we have cast good spells." And she said, "No you aren't." And I said, "Yes, we are." And she said, "No, you aren't." And I said, "Well, why did your mummy call us then?" And she said, "Because my daddy went to fetch the doctor and he was taking too long and my mummy does not want to lose the baby, so she said she will try anything, even from an old witch-woman if it will help." I pinched her and she wailed and her mother shouted out, "What is going on in there?" Then I saw the baby's spirit decide to stay and at the same time the woman started to cry and tell my Nanan to leave her alone, it was all a big mistake and leave immediately or she would have her husband deal with us when he returned. My Nanan wanted our money but there was nothing to be done and we ran home so that we would not be on the street when her husband came around in case he was evil and wanted to harm us and my Nanan was angry at herself for forgetting to cover my head from the dew and she said that if it were not for the ancestors she would give it up. My Nanan says she does it for the ancestors, and for me.

Sometimes other people's mummies come to the window. My Nanan says they never ask for spells to find lost children. They avoid her eyes and ask for spells to make new children lost. My Nanan says she tells them she does not have those kinds of spells but she will try the one to make a bad man stay and do right – and my Nanan says she gives those spells away for free because a woman who needs a spell to make a bad man stay will eventually pay the price of a lifetime.

Sometimes, when we have that type of emergency, my Nanan comes back to bed and holds me oh so tight.

Sometimes, before we sleep, my Nanan and I fly outside of our window and over the barrels and down by a river where the ancestors sit platting their hair on the other side. Sometimes they sing songs to us across the water, sometimes they give us stronger spells or visions or advice, or they warn us about things that are about to happen. Like the time they told my Nanan to sell all her chickens the next day. And she did and people said she was either crazy or retiring and if it was the latter then she was retiring from the wrong thing. But a week after that all the chickens in all the backyards and the farms for miles around caught a sickness and died and their owners lost a lot of money. The ones that weren't saying that my Nanan was one lucky old bat were trying to prove how she killed all those chickens and why. My Nanan kept me indoors for a whole two weeks just to be cautious, but, of course, eventually it all blew over and things went back to normal when a vet from the city came and said it was a disease they caught from a batch of bad feed and couldn't nobody have contaminated it unless they worked at the feed company or had real good connections. Sometimes I hear the ancestors telling my Nanan to come on over and join them. But my Nanan says she will never leave me. And definitely not before I can read the pebbles and hear the wind right.

The time after we came back from the woman who had the dying baby in her belly and the bad daughter, I got sick and my Nanan had to make a spell for me.

"One cup cooling tea for the fever, one cup bush tea to sweat you, two drops olbas oil in your bath water and a hot towel over your head to help you breathe and warm coconut oil drawn in the secret pattern over the chest with a white chicken feather."

That time, I saw everything my Nanan was doing from the other side of the river with the ancestors, and Nanan was crying and asking me how could *I* cross over before she did and what would she do on the other side without me. And I saw her there looking lonely and mournful with the chicken feather. And then my Nanan started to cry and it was her tears that brought me back. 'Cause I reached over the river to wipe them.

And days after that when I was still in bed, though much better – but my Nanan wasn't taking any chances because she says she almost lost me – I said, "Why are you using a feather, Nanan?" And my Nanan said that if she used her hand it would trap the cold inside my chest and it would hide and not come out. And my Nanan said, "Be still and let me catch it all with the feather."

And she did.

On Sunday the postman brought a letter from my mother with a picture in it for me. She is not a star but her lips are just as bright. She is wearing a big smile and a tiny paper hat half-cocked on her hair that says "Big Chicken". The back of the picture says, "First Day of New Job".

"To make a loved one return to you, draw their face in the dust, then take the dust home and put it in a jar facing East. After three days take the jar to a four-cross junction and face West and call the person's name and turn around and throw the dust over your left shoulder.

The next day my Nanan and I are feeding her new chickens. I am walking around picking up the eggs while she calls the birds away from me. That way they will not see me take them. After this we will put the stones she keeps in a red velvet bag in her bosom in a bowl of water. She will watch me take out my own red velvet bag that she sewed for me herself, with my own pebbles and place them into my own bowl of water. My Nanan reads hers first, then mine. And then I read mine. It is hard work hearing the stones. But every day they speak louder. Today it will rain; we will have three clients, all female; their ailments will be of the heart variety so we should pick loveroot and have it ready. And what do they say about you, asks my Nanan. The stones say that today my Nanan will introduce me to a client and let me do the reading and the prescribing.

We will eat noodles today – with saltfish and okra. We will make ourselves new dresses in purple. My Nanan says purple is a good colour for women like us. Women who can listen to the wind and answer the trees and sell for a dollar spells and potions we have pounded ourselves.

BRIDE

Be careful to be nice to him because you are not beautiful. Wear enough make-up to let him think you are beautiful but never so much that he knows you are hiding something.

(Have you brushed your tongue so that your kiss will taste like peppermint?)

Do not kiss him with your tongue in the church or the congregation will think that I have raised you without shame. Do not open your legs too wide tonight or he might think that I forgot to give you virtue. Do not shut them too tight or he will forget his. Here is what to put in his tea if he forgets it anyway.

This is how to draw his tea so it will keep warm enough that he will not taste what you have put into it – just in case he does not come to the table immediately.

(Here, let me press and curl your hair.)

Do not look at other men. Never encourage other men to look at you. Only smile a little when you see his friends and he is not with you. Never smile when you see them and he is. Do not smile too much or he will get suspicious. Do not encourage him to stand still and just look at you. You are not beautiful, but he does not have to find out.

Do not listen to rumours about him and never give anyone any information to fuel rumours about you. Never ask other women where he is or they will laugh at you.

This is how to let him think you are his. You must always go to church to serve your true master. This is how to iron his clothes so that his shirts have no creases. This is how to iron his clothes so that his pants do. This is how to turn his cuckoo. This is how to keep it warm when he keeps you waiting. Always have his dinner waiting so that he will not go out and eat another woman's food. This is what to sprinkle on his pillow if he goes out anyway.

(Pass me the hair-comb to fasten your veil.)

Sometimes he will make you sick. Ignore it and soon you will feel nothing regardless of what he does. This is how his eyes will look when he has a fever. This is what you must bathe him with so he will cool down. This is the leaf you must make into tea to make him feel better. Do not sleep with him when he is sick or you will get sick too and then who will do everything?

(Smoothen your hem.)

Childbirth will threaten to kill you but you will live for your children. Do not let him see you bring his children or they will be the last he will try to make with you. Do not bring too many children or the money he gives you will never be enough. Do not let him spend his money outside of the house. This is what to spray in his pockets if he spends it anyway.

(Where are your flowers?)

Do not linger in bed tomorrow morning or he will think you are lazy. Never wait until the sun rises before you do. Sunlight is a harsh judge of the naked body. Your body was made to be covered. You are not beautiful but you do not have to show it. Always wear a tight bra – even to bed. This is how to pad your bra so that your breasts look fuller. This is how to girdle your ass so it looks smaller. This is how to straighten your hair and this is how often to do it so he does not remember how nappy you can look if you let yourself go. Wear your best panties outdoors in case you fall ill and have to be taken home. Wear your other panties indoors and do not let him see them unless you cannot help it. This is what to do to make sure you do not get pregnant when he cannot afford it. This is how you will feel when you are pregnant. This is how to tell if it will be a girl. This is how to make sure it will be a boy. Never try to get rid of what God has given you after he has given it. This is what to take if you have no choice and these are the prayers to say afterwards to ensure your soul does not go straight to hell.

Do not waste much time on sex. This is how to pretend you are enjoying it. This is how to hide it when you enjoy it too much. This is what to use to get blood out of sheets and panties. Pray for blood on your sheets tonight and in your panties every month that you want it there. If you have taken in my teachings you have nothing to worry about.

(Put your shoes on.)

Berate him privately when he beats the children. Be silent when he beats you. Never hang your dirty laundry in public and never hang your underwear to dry outdoors.

This is how to apply poultice to bruises so the children will not be upset. This is how to apply poultice to your marriage so you will not upset him. This is how to live so your marriage will not upset you. This is how to pray if it does anyway.

(You are ready now. You are not beautiful but I am proud of you.)

This is how you walk up the aisle.

The fallen branches of every tree I have watched grow for the first eighteen years of my life die at my feet as I walk my baby home. My mother is visible through the door to the front room. She is sitting at the kitchen table that, today being wash-day, is naked. She has already scrubbed it with bleach and stripped the wood of colour and texture. It is dull, pale and clean. She is hunched over, elbows on the table, breathing fire into the telephone. Her large legs are spread and her feet are flat on the floor. They are archless, swollen feet – no more than usual – and the cracks of her heels yawn when she shifts her weight from one leg to the other. Her feet are stained by dust. They are so large and grip the ground so firmly that it is hard to imagine her ever having been swept off them. But then she has never claimed to have been swept off them, never admitted to having done anything so frivolous as fall in love.

My mother is eating the assorted left-overs of the past few days. Black pudding stuffed into the taut tyres of pig intestines. Fried flying fish. Breadfruit. Pickled cucumbers. She will say that she hates breadfruit but also that food must not waste. The heads of the fish have been forced open to let the tails come through their mouths like the mocking tongues of cruel children. Their spines have been broken to facilitate the bending, and my mother is contently crunching bone and spitting what cannot be swallowed onto a piece of newspaper in front of her – in between saying something. "For the cat", I imagine.

Through the doorway my mother is remonstrating into the telephone receiver, propped into the fleshy curve of her neck. She keeps glancing at a clock ticking in the belly of Jesus above the kitchen sink. She is wondering whether I will come back, after all, or whether she will have to credit me with being a woman of my word. She looks outside and nods knowingly.

When she comes to the doorway she refers to the last thing I said when I called to say I was pregnant and we argued. She says, "Well, I see you are not dead."

"No, I am not dead," I say.

Against my better judgement I am decidedly alive.

She takes the baby and turns her back to say her good-byes. I step over the threshold as he coos at her, unwary. I go in and close the door. The crook of my arm cools quickly.

"She is here," she says to the telephone before replacing it. She sets a place at the table and to my baby she says, "Come and meet your grandfather."

She goes out the back door which, when opened, lets in the whistle of a machete on greenery. It is the turn of the trees at the back of the house to die. I sit on a chair. It is hard and familiar.

"How was your flight?" he asks when he comes in. He sits behind a plate of hot pudding and cold lemonade that she sets before him. In his glass the ice melts a little and sinks lower in silence. My mother returns to her bones. The baby cries.

"It was alright," I say. "Long."

She pauses from her grinding, "Here," she says. "Or he will think he is mine."

When I take my baby he starts to wail. I try to nurse him but he rejects my breast, looking at me in bewilderment. I am already a stranger.

"He is not hungry," she says, her eyes still on her bones. "He is probably sleepy."

"He has not eaten since we left Heathrow," I dissent, but my voice is weak, plaintive. "He *must* be hungry – he slept all through the flight."

I am rubbing my nipple across his lips. He is turning his head and screaming. My father averts his eyes.

My mother chews her last fish-head thoughtfully and the eyes disappear with two wet slurps of her lips and a sigh. Even with evidence of my womanhood she fears she cannot attribute to me certain womanly talents. She takes the newspaper to the back door and spreads it at her feet. She calls the cat, who waits for her retreat before he approaches his dinner. She washes her hands slowly. She dries them and returns to me on her solid feet. She does everything noisily and between her and the baby I am almost beside myself. When she takes him I am relieved.

"Come to mama," she says to my son, "you poor, sleepy baby. . ."

She starts to sing a nonsense song.

"Big rat had a spree
L'il rat went to see
Big rat take up l'il rat
And throw him in the sea…"

My mother says Big Rat like it is someone that she knows. It could be a neighbour. A friend. It could be she herself. But no image presents itself for L'il Rat. My son's eyes start to close and his writhing stills with her patting. It is her manner more than her method that he responds to. She is the woman of this house. When I became as infantile as he is he did not know me.

"You are looking like your Aunty Sissy," she says to me in the new silence. "Dads, don't she favour Sissy?"

66

My father scrutinizes my face like he would a picture of a remote relative.

"A little," he says.

My mother smirks.

"But Sissy run to fat. She don't work as hard as I do. All she do is have babies for foolish men."

She looks hard at me.

"What is it you were studying again, before this. . . ?"

"Voice, I was training my voice to be a singer."

It had been a bone of contention in its day – before it became negligible in the face of an illegitimate baby. Who in their right mind travelled thousands of miles and borrowed money to learn how to sing? Singing was not something that people needed. You could not eat it, wear it or use it to live. Who studies something that you either can or cannot do? Only someone idiot enough to turn around spoil it all by having a baby without the security of a husband.

"Your song is probably too sweet," says my mother.

"Some girls cannot tell the difference between a man who wants to help her sing a song and a man who just wants to hear it," says my father.

"Finish your food," says my mother.

My father gulps the last of his lemonade, the ice so small he swallows it all with one quiet motion. It makes no sound on its way into his throat. He returns to the murder of the garden.

My mother tells me that he started to axe the trees since I called and told them I was taking a year off college to come home with the baby. It has been three days and they are almost all gone. The mammy-apple, the breadfruit, the cherry will henceforth be referred to in the past tense. She starts to sing a hymn. A requiem for the departed.

She is removing my father's setting with one hand and holding my baby with the other. She has rendered me useless and I take as long as I can to replace my breast.

67

"Your old friend Mellie has gone to Cuba," she informs. "On scholarship to study Doctor-work."

Loosely translated it would read something like, "Mellie is making something of her life and learning something people can use."

We are momentarily lost in our private thoughts. But we speak at the same time.

"She will probably come back home soon with a Cuban baby."

"That's good. Mellie's very bright."

"What?" she asks, with her eyes flashing.

My father's pyrex bowl has fallen but is not shattered. The noise starts the baby crying again.

"About the scholarship," I say.

I take my baby from her arms and put him over my shoulder. She eyes my hold on him with doubt. I pat him and he burps and then he settles down again. When he does she sucks her teeth as if she has already forgotten about Mellie. She is singing her hymn again. It may be for herself.

"Come," she says to us, quietly, "let me show you where to put him down."

She goes up the stairs on her solid feet, the cracks of her ankles yawn with each step.

I am home.

A DAY OF DELIVERANCE

I ain't really want to kill Carson.

Maybe just hurt him a little bit.

Sometimes you get fed up, you know. Sometimes you get tired of the same old routine. Sometimes, when you getting old and saggy in all the wrong places, and your stretch marks singing the Hallelujah chorus that they finally free and making tracks all over your body – so that even you don't want to see it – sometimes, well, sometimes you just need a man to come home to love you regardless.

But my Carson is a kinda man.

Carson gone over and aways, says he working on a farm in Canada. He does come back maybe three times a year, flashing gold from tooth to toe-nail, and when I ask him about all that money I hear they be making up in Canada, when I ask Carson about that money and if is true he spending it on that woman I hear he have up there, Carson does get mad, mad, mad and say who I am to ask him about his money, far less how he is to spend it and who he is to spend it on, and before I know it his hand done fly up and hit me in the face, and is a while before he stop. Hitting me, Ethelene Elvira Ransom, even now after I been forty-nine long years on God's good earth.

My Carson is a kinda man.

But tonight I waiting for him.

Waiting with my pipe smoking and a cup of bush tea to kill the hurt in my stomach – which maybe is more from the knowledge that he could hit me than from any damage he done with his fist, but it hurt all the same. Waiting with my feet in an enamel basin of Epsom salt water because look like this time he maybe broke a toe. Waiting on our bed with a scissors under my behind. Lord forgive me. Waiting for that old ribsy, yellow-belly dog to come through the door and strip down to his BVDs and try to play bedroom bully.

Somebody going to show who is bully tonight.

Somebody going jump right out of this raggedy house he put me and the children in, with the broken-down verandah he shoulda fix, the leaky roof he pretend to fix and the pain in my stomach he can't fix.

But I going fix him, though. And soon.

My Carson is a kinda man.

Carson come in at a quarter of four, chupsing and trying to figure out which one of the five belts he seeing is the one actually holding up his pants. Carson smiling. Carson singing. Carson saying,

"Ethie, dou-dou, come help me, nuh?"

Carson smiling and I know he thinking I done come to my senses cause I ain't saying a word and I smiling right back at him. I smiling on my back, watching ghosts climb out of my pipe and kiss the roof that bleeding rain into the buckets I had to put on the floor. And I'm thinking to myself, Lord, I am so tired of this, Lord, I am so very tired. And I mighta not done it, but when Carson dropped in the bed and I smelt the alcohol on him, I push him off me with my free hand and I started praying for forgiveness in advance 'cause I done seen his arm descending on my face and my scissors' hand wasn't mine no more. Just like that I seen that scissors make a hole in Carson's yellow behind.

I seen Carson start digging his thumbs into the mattress and I seen his lips opening and closing like one of Johnson guppies gasping for air and I seen Carson's mouth open real wide and, though I couldn't hear him, I knew he was bawling "MURDER!" and I seen the children come running into the bedroom, upsetting my buckets, and I thinking I wonder if I got enough towels to wipe up that mess when they done making it, and then I heard somebody crying and I seen Carson run outside with red rivers running down the backs of his legs.

"Mama, you alright?"

Was Pet. She's my youngest and although she getting breasts she still got her baby face. My hand come back to me then and I put the scissors in a drawer.

"Yes, honey, mama's fine."

Is Daddy that going have a little problem.

Dear Aunt Clothilda round the door-frame with dawn, hawking sleep from her chest and tickling her gums with her tongue the way she does when her teeth on secondment to a jam jar of water. Clothilda is Carson old auntie. She don't really talk to me too much. She so old (Carson say she is over 102) I not even sure she remember how to talk – she mostly sing spirituals all day long. And the song she sing will tell you how she feeling. When she not singing we have to check and make sure she not dead.

"Is alright, Dear Aunt," I tell her.

Clothilda start to sing "Nearer my God to Thee".

Everybody have to know that she upset.

When I get home from work most days, I just tired, you know.

In the kitchen, Pet on the floor next to the stove, sitting on a fold-up chair cushion. (Lord, Pet, that is my good chair cushion you put on the floor?)

Pet got Vaseline in her right hand and the left she using to separate the fuzzy hair from what Nora already burn straight. Nora pretty fingers turn red from the heat and they holding the hot iron like they 'fraid it and Pet looking like she ain't too sure why she let Nora press her hair in the first place.

Tonight home smell like burning hair and petroleum jelly and rain and baby diapers and wet chickens.

(And Nora, why you ain't making those children close the back door from those chickens running in outta the rain?)

Pet twin, Betsy, waiting for Nora to hurry up and finish so she could get hers done in time to style off by Smitty squawky-voice son and Connie (she my eldest baby-mother) breast-feeding little Johnson at the table. All of them talking over the hair sizzling and the peas boiling and the chickens complaining and the Rediffusion spouting the Bible.

Some days you just tired, you know.

And today my back aching too 'cause I had to polish the floors at Miss Vincent's place. Let me tell you, them floors ain't easy. You ever had to clean a house from top to bottom that wasn't yours and to feed some dogs that does try they very best to bite the blasted hand that feeding them (and you have to do it even though everybody that know you know you ain't no dog-lover) and to make things for other people dinner that you could never afford for your own family? You ever had to wait around in a kitchen till other people finish the dinner that you make for them so you could get a ride to the bus stop to try and get home to eat yours? You ever had to take the bus when it raining bad and you does get sick easy if you not careful and the same people that leave you at the bus stop ain't paying you enough to afford another doctor-bill this month, and Mr. Vincent not even saying, "Let me drop you to your house, Ethelene, seeing as it raining, and is just a few miles in a car and you don't ever ask me for a ride, so today I am going to offer you one."

When I get home it still raining, and it raining so bad that I hearing it rain inside my head even when I come inside and close the door to the world and the noise in the house supposed to drown it out.

"Mama, don't forget graduation is next month, you know."

I light my pipe and start looking for the Epsom salts leisurely, like I ain't in no hurry to find it 'cause I can't let myself keep quiet long enough to study another expense.

"You fit the dress at Marjorie?"

"Yeah, she say it'n cost you fifty dollars."

"For you and Betsy?"

"No, each."

I take a good long draw on the pipe and ease in a chair and put my feet in the water. They big and brown and wide and the toes look like they permanently curling under to grip the ground those times when I sure I can't stand any more and they still hold me up. Sometimes I need to look at them feet just to make sure I still upright.

I look at Pet. She young. She vibrant. She have too many dreams in eyes that don't see "can't" and can't see money. And if there is one thing I learn in life is that most dreams mean money. But her feet soft and tender and pretty and smooth and sometimes I promise myself that they ain't never going to look like mine if I have anything to do with it. I does try – for her. She saying the welcome at the graduation.

"You see the dress, Nora?"

Nora is the quietest of my brood and the best thing that come from Carson side of the family. She ain't really mine – her mother is some white German woman Carson take up with one time that make his baby and left it for him. Nora come to live with us when she was almost two. Nora is the colour of milky tea and she have big cat eyes that look like the sky when it rain for days – and just as solemn – and she have straightened brown hair past her shoulders that does catch the sun and play with it. She does make old men wish they was young again when she pass them. And my Nora had some men. Black men. White men. Businessmen. Politicians. The only kind of man Nora never had was a poor man. Nora is a perfume girl in a posh department store in town and not a day goes by that she don't smell like one of the best samples in Ms. Vincent's magazines. Nora does dress up pretty pretty pretty in the clothes the men does give her.

I ask Nora because she is the one with the sense of style.

"It's very nice, Mum," she say.

I ain't have to tell you that my Nora does talk smooth so all the time. Carson like to tell her that she belong reading the evening news on TV. But Nora say she looking to be an air hostess. Nora been thinking that ever since she start dating the pilot-man.

"Nice?" Pet squealing and getting excited and causing the pressing-iron to fall off the flame. "We copy it from one of Nora fashion-book, Mama. It have organza ruffles across the hips and a low neck and no sleeves and…"

I try to look strict.

"It sounding much too grown to me!"

Connie baby make a clucking noise when he release her breast and start to bellow like we talking too hard for him to concentrate on what he doing.

"Is secondary school you leaving, Pet, and that is how you supposed to look – like a young lady leaving school," I explain.

Pet get quiet and crestfallen. But I going let her wear whatever the hell she want to – I just don't want her to look too old and wise. Sometimes I just want to hold on to these children as they are now. Other times I wish they would all grow and get out of my house and leave me to hell alone. Now I gotta figure out what I'm going to leave out to get the $100 to buy them their dresses.

Dear Aunt Clothilda shuffle in and give everyone a nasty look and start singing "Thy Way Not Mine Oh Lord", while she make her tea. And Connie start threatening Johnson with a slap if he don't shut up and Betsy start shouting 'cause Nora finally burn her with the pressing comb and the kitchen start breathing again and I just staying quiet 'cause

74

I so tired and I can't bother with thinking about the business of the dress right now.

Without even Carson few pennies since I stab him and he gone back in aways (and his side of the family cutting they eyes at me and saying how lucky I am that Carson ain't press no charges, and they did always know that I ain't no good anyhow); and with Johnson Senior finishing up his two years for breaking and entering and coming home soon (but he ain't really do it, he just unlucky) and coming to be another mouth for me to feed 'cause I know with a record a job for him going to be hard to come by; and with Connie looking like she making baby again (even though Johnny wasn't home – but that ain't my business) I feeling for money in the worst way.

On Sunday, I at home in the middle of the quiet with my papers and my pipe. I make everybody go to church on a Sunday and I tell them they need it. Me, I past salvation – and in any event I have to stay home and cook and clean when nobody can get in my way and I can make peace with the rest of the week. And besides (but I don't tell them this) I don't want to meet up with that ugly soprano that Carson does take up with when he come back, 'cause, Lord help me, I might hurt her too. Right now my bills and my troubles overtaking me – and not even a man to turn around to.

Is then I see the advert in the paper for the cooking class the Hospitality Institute having. "Culinary Arts & Catering Management". Three months. A certificate. And experience will do if you don't have "O" levels. After forty-nine years on God's great earth I ain't never get no certificates. Maybe that piece of paper will put Mrs. Vincent's mind at rest so she can sit down and leave me in peace when I polishing her silver instead of pretending to help me when I know she have other things to do. Maybe it will let her get out of my kitchen (even if it is hers) when I am cooking for her parties and she is all in a fluster and questioning if I ain't putting in too much of this or that. Maybe it will even get me another job, somewhere I can earn enough to tell Carson to keep his lazy behind in Canada if he want to, I can take care of everything just by myself. And I smile. Sometimes it look like the good Lord does pay home visits.

The gate groan and I had to check and see it wasn't Clothilda (she don't go to church either 'cause the walk is too much for her and she mostly fall asleep anyways) 'cause sometimes Clothilda does walk away and last time we find her in the funeral dress Carson did bring back from aways ('cause she was sick and we did swearing that she couldn't have much longer to go) and there she was smiling without her teeth and singing "All Things Bright & Beautiful" with some drunkard at Delbert's bar, showing everybody her underwear and drinking brandy.

But is the others back from church.

"Clothilda," I holler, to make sure she still breathing.

And she start up with "When Peace Like A River".

When he come out I almost ain't recognize Johnnie. Only Connie used to visit really, 'cause I couldn't get off from work most times and nobody else wasn't really that fussing about going. Me and Nora and the twin went in this posh taxi that I beg Carson for the money to hire, and I wear my Donna Summer wig and my best orange dress with the steam-pleat pockets and the white shoes and the pearls to match. But when Johnnie walk out the green iron gates they had him locked behind, it ain't look like he been getting the foodstuff I sent him 'cause he lost at least the fat he went in with and probably more – and he wasn't no prized pig to begin with, he skinny just like his father. I trying not to cry.

"You alright, Johnnie?"

"I glad to see y'all, Mama," he say.

And then I hug him and he look like he ain't want to move

off my bosom, and although he squeezing me hard enough to flatten the wig and the steam-pleats, I let him. Even though Connie there, is me he stay hugging and is only when we get home that he really kiss her and they went into their room and I play with Johnson junior to give them a little time to get reacquainted.

Everything was fine after that till Nora come home one day and announce that she leaving the next to stay in Antigua with the pilot-man and train to turn air hostess. As soon as I hear that I had to light my pipe.

"How long you going for, Nora?" I ask her. 'Cause once Nora done make up her mind in her quiet way it don't make no sense trying to sway her. Best to let her make her own mistakes in her own good time.

"I'm not sure, Mum, but I'll stop-over whenever I can."

Lord, the child was just two years old at my knee, looking at me with her cat-eyes and trying to see if she could trust me and now she telling me 'bout she going "stop-over". And Carson ain't here to tell her 'bout her family and how she belong to us, just as sure as I make her like I make Pet and Betsy and Johnson, and how she don't belong with no pilot-man who ain't going married her when all said and done and who ain't ever going to love her like we love her.

I feeling like this dog Carson had. A real slutty dog, it was; puppies as soon as you turn around, but Carson just used to pick up those puppies and give them away one by one while the dog watch him – until the dog just pick up one day and give Carson a dirty look and left and never came back. I didn't blame it then and nobody can't blame me now for feeling like I make something, and somebody, who ain't bear no pain for it, just take it away like is nothing. And though I ain't make Nora like I make Pet and Betsy and Johnson, I still feeling that way.

Nora standing in front of the wardrobe the Furniture-Store-Manager-man did give her and she dividing the clothes she can't take with her between Connie and Pet and Betsy and packing the things she want to keep and telling us about the uniform the air hostesses does wear. Pet screaming delight at every new thing Nora give her, Connie trying on a silk shirt and Betsy making plans for what new thing she going wear by Smitty squawky-voice son later on. I just there wondering how to let Nora go and who going tell me which colours to go with what skirt and how I must not put perfume behind my ears, how I must spray it above my head and let it rain on me "just like a cloud, Mum, just like a cloud".

Is when she press some real diamond earrings that the lawyer-friend did give her in my palm (he turn out to be married) that I start to cry. Nora make the others leave and we just sit in her room holding each other and crying until it was all out and she let them come in again and this time Clothilda was with them. Nora give Clothilda a perfume so expensive you might think it was made with gold dust in it, but Clothilda just wander back out of the room holding it so slack between her fingers I thought she might drop it. She ain't even suffer Nora a kiss goodbye and I wasn't sure she appreciate that Nora was about to be gone, but the night after Nora left I hear her spraying something in her potty and the next morning she wouldn't let me empty it 'cause it had her room smelling just like Nora.

Classes coming along alright, you know.

I sure I know more about cooking than that bird-voice, no-breast, Bible-cover-black girl they have teaching it (imagine she trying to tell me, Ethelene Elvira Ransom, the difference between a fish fork and a salad fork and scolding me for not remembering – even though she young enough for me to put her over my knee) but two more weeks and I be getting my first certificate. A paper with my name on it. At fifty years old.

Pet and Betsy graduation was good. Clothilda put on my

Chaka Khan wig and Nora old peach push-alongs and her funeral dress to see my two youngest get their first certificates and try as we might she wouldn't let us take anything off her. Me and Clothilda and Johnnie and Connie sit in the front row (I had to make them leave Baby Johnson by the neighbour 'cause Connie so big now she can hardly manage him and I didn't want him crying and spitting up and making me miss anything important).

Pet and Betsy hair was grease-down real nice and shiny and Pet flouncy dress did look spectacular up there on the stage when she was giving her welcome and when she finish I run up and give her a kiss – although they say, "Parents, please stay off the stage until the end of the ceremony", and even the Government Minister was clapping for her. Afterwards I give she and Betsy each a five to buy ice cream – 'cause I was so happy I forget I might need it to buy milk or flour or something and none of us remember to feel bad 'cause Carson and Nora ain't make it. We get a letter from Nora with some money for the girls that I put away for when they getting the next certificates. She say that she and the pilot-man down. She dating the Airport Manager now. She say she might marry this one.

When we get home, Connie and Johnnie go to collect the baby and Pet and Betsy go for their ice cream and Carson call collect to say that he lonely and he miss us, an after he almost get run over by a tractor on the farm, an after he see an angel that pick him up in the nick of time, he find the Lord and when this contract finish he coming back home to be a good man.

My Carson is a kinda man.

I say, "Carson, you just expect me to believe that you change your ways overnight?"

And he say no, but he will prove it to me when he come. He say he love me. Which is something I ain't heard him say in over twenty years.

Well, I cut him off short ('cause things still ain't easy and he calling collect and he ain't say he going pay for the call), but I say I will talk to him again soon, and I get out my basin and fill it up with Epsom salt-water and put in my feet and light up some fresh tobacco.

I think about Clothilda.

"Dear Aunt, you alright?"

And Clothilda start, "I'll Meet You In The Morning. . ."

Then I remember that tomorrow is my birthday. And I'm going to get me a new pipe and perhaps a new wig. Seen a lady at the graduation in one that look like Whitney Houston and I think it'd suit me...

LUTHER

I cannot tell Luther that his song has failed to convince a panel of three student judges that it deserves airplay in the Students' Union and five hundred dollars. He probably cannot remember much human, and I certainly do not speak cat. In any event, the news would likely break his heart. I do not wish to deprive Luther of any of his lives.

The night he wrote the song we were lying on our backs in the banana patch by the Natural Sciences laboratory. We had been talking about the experiments they do on plants and how they were probably growing something on the bananas, just to see if they could kill it afterwards. We were smoking two joints we had made from a five-bag we had bought from the man in a box on the beach. Luther had gone to the side of the box where Understanding had drawn two Crayola red windows and a door.

"Understanding," Luther said, "a five-bag."

"Ah-h-h-h," exhaled Understanding through mist, as if he truly did. "Let me see the five."

He peered at us from the top of the box through a pair of binoculars Luther said he'd gotten from a cereal box. Understanding has a snatching habit. He's like a crow and as black. He keeps everything in the box, which moves from spot to spot on the beach depending on his whims and the weather. He reached for our money.

"The weed," said Luther, dangling the bill in the air.

Understanding cut his one good eye, chupsed, traced the gold of his teeth and flung at Luther our oblivion for that night. Luther passed the money over the top of the box.

In the banana patch Luther smoked the last of his joint and strummed Itesey. Itesey was the guitar we had found in a gully and painted ites, gold and green.

"Me ital," he intoned, with the loftiness of the discoverer of a truism, "is vital."

And he sang while I scrambled to write it down, as it flowed from his mouth, on one of the papers in my knapsack.

I could not explain how that song did not win to a new cat.

"Luther," I say instead, "we will be late for our meeting."

Luther meows. He has been smoking with me all morning and I have to shake him fully awake, to his great annoyance. He was dozing in my handbag with his feet crossed. I imagine he must have liked my bag while he still walked on two legs, so easily did he take to it after he learned to purr and I could carry him.

The Principal does not want to let "a cat" into our meeting.

"Luther will not cause a disturbance," I tell him. "And it's not like you two have never met." As a matter of fact, Luther has always been very quiet when he is high. I see no reason why things should change because he has fur.

The Principal insists.

"You are treating him like a stranger!" I say, through tears. "And after he has washed your car so faithfully for so long."

I insist there will be no meeting without Luther. The Principal eyes him as he says that he has spoken to the school board and they have agreed to send me on administrative leave, for rest. Luther, according to his meowing, is not a bit surprised.

Two weeks ago, without a tail, he had said, "Saunders

(which is what he called me), why you don't tell the boss-man to kiss your rass?"

"It wouldn't be right," I told him, twisting his locks with the tips of my fingers.

"Right, shite," said Luther, rolling a joint, "He din' pass you over for another promotion? He ain't always confusing you and vexing yuh spirit?"

"Well, you wash his car, Luther," I protested, "and you never told him to kiss your rass."

"Boss-man never do me nothing," said Luther.

The Principal is not unlike a large rat. His mouth furls in on itself. His eyes are like pinheads – and as bright. Were his moustache any wider it would make him whiskers. I am thinking that now Luther is a cat he will finally avenge me. But Luther is sleeping with his mouth open, drooling onto my cheese sandwich. The Principal hands me a memo to take three months' leave.

"Your students are beginning to talk," he says solemnly.

"I did not know they had it in them," I reply.

Luther and I leave.

The day that I discovered Luther's Great Transformation was the day after I watched a maxi-taxi knock him dead on Broad Street. He had been standing by his brother's coconut cart, helping him split nuts and empty their water into bottles for tourists. He had seen me and went to cross the street to where I was standing. There was a screech, and Luther lay still on the ground.

I had been with my husband, on our way to buying something he thought we needed. He came over to look at Luther. He said that the government needed to do something about these rasta men selling coconuts so close to the curbs. They were a danger to themselves and other road users. Look what has happened to this one. I heard him from far away. Somebody called the ambulance. On the ground Luther looked like a stranger. My husband pulled me away. Luther's brother watched me leave like I was vermin, but acted like he did not know me.

At home that night my husband wondered why I was crying. He fielded my calls. He told my sister that I had witnessed a death on the street and it had upset me. He told his friend, Shane, that I was shaken to the core by a senseless fatality that had occurred right in front of my eyes. He made me camomile tea and put me to bed, where I sat up while he slept, hearing birds screaming good-mornings.

I had been up thinking that I did not recognize the body in the street as one with which I had once shared an intimate connection. I had been up thinking that I had not recognized it at all.

The next morning my husband insisted that I stayed at home but I drove to the car park anyway, expecting to see Luther in his familiar spot, hunched over the left rear wheel of the Principal's Audi, giving the hub-cap a spit-shine. Instead, he was licking the wheel, flicking a long ginger tail, getting accustomed to life as a tabby.

"Luther," I called. And he had run to me immediately and sniffed my bag. After we were reunited I had put him inside my bag. He has been there ever since.

"Luther," I said that night in the banana patch, when he had started to tell me about his life as a thief before he had found Jah, "Luther, why don't you just leave this place and go somewhere where your songs will be appreciated?"

He told me he had cancer, for which he was being treated at the hospital. Getting over it was his first priority. He said it that way – "getting over it" – and then he said that he would go, if I would go with him.

"I couldn't, Luther," I had said. "What would I tell my husband? Who would teach my students?"

"Tell them all you love me," said Luther.

We kissed then, and after we laughed at the headiness of it.

"But seriously," I had said. "They love reggae in Europe."

"You wan' get rid o' me?" asked Luther.

"You could make money," I said.

"Money for wha'?" asked Luther. "You have money and it do you any good?"

Luther started to strum Itesey, "Money is funny, honey," he began, and waited for me to write it down.

When my husband went away on business trips, I relocated to Luther's shack in the gully. He had built it himself with bits of branch, galvanize and assorted pieces of plywood and clapboard. We slept on the floor with the door open to the density of trees and bush, deepened and made mysterious by the noise of the rain, the night, the animals. We slept naked, with our arms around each other and when it was time for me to go to the toilet, Luther got up and lit a lantern to guide me to a hole he dug for me, and stood and watched me squat and walked me back and wrapped me up in his arms again. He did not seem to think there was anything unusual about the way we lived in the gully. We roasted sweet potatoes and plantains on open fires and cooled our coconut water in an ice-box he powered with a car battery. And we talked all the time.

Once I visited Luther in hospital when I came to work and found his nephew washing the Audi and he told me where he was. I stood by his bedside and sneaked him a joint I had gotten only after Understanding had snatched three of my five-dollar bills. I cried when I saw the colourless shift they had him in and that they had shaved and washed him. Even his nails were clean and clipped. The joint looked strange against his scrubbed lips, his de-bushed face, his bald head. He had had an operation. He said the doctors had told him the prognosis was grim.

"I is more worried about *you*," he said, when he saw my expression.

"But I am not dying," I said.

"Give it time," said Luther. Then he started to sing a song about dying. I did not try to scribble it down. His voice was weak and trod without certainty over lips so cold and clean. His song suddenly sounded like something you laugh at.

"Make sure they cremate I-man," said Luther. "They could give the ashes to Understanding." He laughed at his own joke, holding the spliff between trembling fingers. I did not know then that it would be our last.

"But how can I reduce you to ashes?"

"I am more worried about you," Luther said again, but he had almost finished the spliff and he might have forgotten that he'd said that already.

We talked about the Carnival competition on campus and Luther said he had entered and I applauded and Luther said he might as well get something for his singing now, because he might not make it to Europe after all. Luther was killed three days later.

The winning song is better than Luther's. As he passes the Students' Union in my handbag on our way to three months' respite, we are both silent in the jangle of the catchy calypso. The winning song is about a mad English professor in love with a car-washing rasta man.

"I will miss you the way you were before the transformation," I whisper in Luther's ear, once we are in the car, "but I will love you regardless."

Luther is silent as I light us a new joint.

THE BURNING BUSH WOMEN

ENEN

My name was Enen Bush and I was the product of a mad mother, a bad man who was good to me and too many children who unintentionally tore me down. This I tried to tell each of them at various times in my life, but they did not hear me. I often tried to tell Jesus, but I have no proof that he heard me either.

I could not figure myself out in the presence of any of them, so I mostly walked through the canefields to think about my life. From all accounts, Jesus spoke to people on their way to or from somewhere – as he did to Paul. I walked more miles of cane than I care to remember, and it still did not come clear to me. On reflection, it was perhaps because, for all my walking, I had no destination in mind. My feet just followed the cane.

Which may be why, when I returned from my walks and was confronted with my children, I had no answers.

Which may be why my last walk ended with as many questions as it began.

FEMI

We live by our hair.

It never lies.

We welcome rain when our plaits undo of their own volition and retreat into themselves. We are pregnant when our hair turns the colour of beetroot and are about to die when it lies still against our scalps and becomes straight and starts to drain itself of its fire. We are sick when it refuses to be ignited by sunlight.

It is not only the hair of the affected Bush that speaks when something is about to happen.

Our hair speaks to all of us.

The Bush women sit for hours in descending clusters at Dear Bush's house on every given Friday, after the last strains of the new soap have expired on Dear Bush's Sony. We bend, hand-deep in the heads of snakes we grow and tame ourselves, winding out of them all the sorrow and stress of a week past and kneading in a familiar and soothing neatness.

We are generally tall and shaped like avocados, with hips our midwives agree were made for child-bearing, and breasts that sit in dots on our chests despite the best coaxings of our men. We have large hands, large feet, and are prone to nervousness – but you tell us by our hair. Mostly it is fuzzy, often thick and tangled, but always, always, it is red. Blood-red, fire-red, burning-bush-atop-your-head red.

We have jointly and severally singed it, dyed it and lye-fried it.

It is never consumed.

Which is why we submit at Dear Bush's on Fridays, lulled by the Sony, sharing our Scotch, our cigars, our secrets and our hair. When we leave, our scalps are usually exposed in shining networks of parts and plaits. Pinned under. Because Bush women never let their hair hang low.

Many days I cried on the toilet. The children had already learnt that the bathroom was personal to me. It was the only place they would let me be. They sought to roll over and tumble under and talk to and touch and taunt and hurt and hug me everywhere in the house but there. When I went there they turned to Madonna.

There were eight steps to my bathroom. Sometimes there were nine and I had to do them over again. There were four steps to the toilet – if I was about to have an accident, and six when I could take my time. I used four sheets of paper for big jobs and one for small ones. Sometimes the paper separated other than at the serrated edge and I used none at all. There were seven steps to the bathtub, six back to the light and three to close the door. Sometimes when I mis-stepped and continued I could still hear counting in my head when I reached my bed. It ticked at me from under my covers until I had to repeat it – properly – so I could get some rest.

I was sitting in streaming water when I saw a spider crabbing along the edge of the flecked enamel. He was not spinning a web. There were no fine gossamer threads to anchor him to anything real. My hair told me this was an omen. The spider crawled across three tiles from the time I first noticed him until the time he finally reached the slippery surface of the tub. The steam rose and changed into water that sweated off my face and into my bathwater. Sometimes the fog made it difficult to see the spider.

I was almost faint from the heat.

The spider was black with many white marks that defied counting.

And then Melkey called my name.

From a far-off place under the water. He sounded afraid. Surprised. The water did not rush off me as I jumped up. It tried to keep me under.

"Melkey," I said. When the water finally released me there was no answer, just the soft sound of liquid sliding off my skin and onto the tiles, being slapped and squashed by the soles of my feet. "Melkey?"

The opening of my front door brought a chill that never left. The drops on my shoulders turned cold and unfriendly and disappeared.

Melkey was on his face in the African violets. His fingers clutched their leaves as if he wished to steady himself while the earth shook. His eyes glazed over right after he looked at me. The doctors said it was a massive heart attack. He could not have survived it whole. His friends were surprised. He was a fit and able cane-cutter with a muscular pair of caramel-coloured arms that he protected from cane-cuts with layers and layers of clothing. Some neighbours felt that he had received his comeuppance. I was numb.

It was after that that I started the walking. It seemed like I either spent my days in the bathtub, trying to hear Melkey. Or walking, trying to find him. At all times I would be crying.

On the days that I cried on the toilet, the children would stand outside the door. Quietly, but I knew they were there because I could hear their feet shuffling. At other times I would hear a timid knock, which would come to me under the water. And moments later one pair of feet would run and return with another.

On the days that I cried in the cane nobody heard me, although Madonna sometimes came looking for me.

When Madonna opened the door to the bathroom, the children would run off because she shooed them. She did not want them to see me in the state I was in, which I now recognize as an act of kindness. The children, having forgotten me, would get up to some mischief while she entered the bathroom and closed the door behind her. Her red stilettos would stop near the tub after twelve steps and I would wonder whether she knew that she almost always did exactly twelve. She would retrieve and shake a thermometer twice, although we both knew damn well that I had no temperature. I was already cold-blooded. Her arms were sluggish and they jangled with the weight of her bangles. There were twenty-four on each arm. I had often counted them.

Madonna never tried to remove me unless I was under water. She mostly sat on the covered toilet and watched me, rocking her red patent-leather shoes back and forth, toes to heels, heels to toes. Her big toes turned grotesquely away from each other. Her littler toes were long and multi-jointed. Like monkey toes. Her shoes had seven pairs of eyes through which red ribbon snaked taut to contain her large feet.

She sometimes wondered aloud whether I wished for some soup. I never did. Sometimes I would not eat for days. Looking and listening for Melkey took so much of my time and energy that it seemed that, mentally, I could deal with nothing else requiring any exertion of memory or even the simplest decision.

She let the water flow sometimes until my slightest movement threatened to send it careening over the edge and towards her shoes. Then she would reach up and turn off the tap.

One day Madonna said, "I am sorry if his death makes you also want to die."

Water is beautiful. It cannot be counted. It adopts the shape of the thing that holds it together. Without that thing, it falls apart.

That is why I sometimes crawled beneath it and tried to stay there.

FEMI

It was our hair that told us, though we did not know it at the time.

That particular Friday night, there we were, squatting, sitting, sprawled under tufts of red Bush hair that suddenly started to lay straight. I saw it first, standing as I was behind the Sony, towards which all the Bush heads were turned, trying to get the picture right. Taja Bush was saying, "More to the right, Femi," and I was moving the aerial but abandoned it in the middle of a bad picture, staring at our hair. Then Dear Bush started to moan because even the parts we had made into plaits were already flat, as if we had ironed them.

We counted ourselves and found none of us missing, so we worried which of us was dying unbeknownst to herself. That in itself was a puzzle, because our hair always talks before a death. It was inconceivable that it was capable of lying.

On that night, Dear Bush turned off the Sony and moaned the old songs in a language most of us had long forgotten. We finished our hair in that moaning quiet, punctuated by the click-clack of our fingernails meeting each other, so that when Dear Bush broke for breath, the silence was a sudden intrusion.

For the first time our hair was a puzzle.

ENEN

I dyed my hair jet black and cut it right to the scalp soon after I moved in with Melkey. I cut my hair because I did not wish to risk it speaking to me. It sometimes spoke anyway. I cut my hair as a sign of mourning, too. It was my one allowance of the Bush ways. I cut my hair soon after Melkey had acknowledged his love for a woman besides Madonna and me. She was a fishmonger from the market, whom I had never seen before, although Melkey said that she had seen me. I had always known that there had been others. But he had never professed to love any of them.

He was distraught when my wrap fell away one night to reveal a shiny black scalp, illuminated by the candles that lit our room. One of the few things Melkey did tell me was that he loved my hair, spreading around my face like an unruly red fan while I was beneath him. He was so shocked he spoke gibberish.

"Your hair," Melkey said. "Where is your hair?"

"I cut it off," I told him.

"But so low? You look like you are ill," said Melkey.

"Perhaps," I said.

Melkey said nothing.

Melkey had moved me and my children into the house he shared with his wife after I told him that Dear Bush had disowned me because I had vowed to her face to stay with him. This was not strictly true. From the time I was eighteen – there were two children then – Dear Bush would shove a mirror into my face at the hair-gathering every Friday.

"Look," she would say. "He is draining you of your spirit. I know the hair has told you."

I used to sit between her thighs, feeling her yank my head in her anger, while the boys ran around the living room.

One evening, I said I would not suffer any longer her insulting Melkey, who loved me, otherwise I would leave her house. Dear Bush said she would speak as she wished about Melkey, who was incapable of loving anyone, considering his record of trying to love so many.

So I left.

Now I realize that it had nothing to do with Dear Bush. It was another of those things I had done to get Melkey to say the things I wished to hear. To say the things he did not tell me. The things that would assure me that he did not *not* say them, just so he could never be accused of lying.

The day he moved me in, I saw his wife, on my way in from the garage, standing over a box of plates. She had drawn a red line across the floor of the doorway that separated the front rooms from the bedrooms and had built a makeshift kitchen in the backyard. She had also started laying bricks across the division but had stopped at waist level and sometimes she used to stand behind the bricks and watch the daily machinations of our lives from the backrooms without saying a word.

I never looked directly at her.

In half-glances and cat-eyes I gathered she was short and Asian, with a peculiar fondness for wearing a pair of high-heeled, red-ribboned boots as she went about her business through the house. My ears told me that she was talkative when among friends, probably humorous – an animated speaker by the exclamations of her many bracelets. My nose told me that she was partial to jasmine scents and cooked with many mysterious spices.

One night, after we made love, Melkey told me her name was Madonna.

He also told me that she could not have children.

FEMI

It was only afterwards, in the quiet sweeping-up of shed Bush hair and the retrieval and replacement of wide-toothed combs and open jars of grease that it came to me. There was another Bush woman who had not been accounted for. A Bush woman who no longer spoke to her hair or her family.

Dear Bush had led us all to the funeral, shrouded in black,

with our heads covered, when Melkey died. Underneath our veils our hair was tightly wrapped. It would not do to let it be seen at a death. But at the same time, it would have been hypocritical to shave our heads for Melkey. He was not one of us by blood or union. We were there only because of Enen. And as things stood, we could not shave our heads for her either.

Enen did not speak to us. Apparently Melkey's wife had made all the arrangements. Enen seemed to have just turned up to take her place among the mourners – in the front pew, next to Madonna. They all sat together: Enen, Madonna, the fishmonger, the woman from up the road, the shopkeeper, the laundry-girl. They sat together and poured their tears on themselves without animosity for each other or for the man whose love they had knowingly shared. There was a buzz about that, a muted wave of murmured surprise from the black-suited grouping, many of whom had attended with the hope they would display their ignorance of each other.

Enen was the only woman who was quiet.

She did not speak. She did not sing. She did not sob.

The Bush women sat together at the wake, save one, in Melkey's living room and watched a swimming silver plate of tiny sandwiches, kept buoyant by one brown hand after another, navigate the crowd of people who sat and talked and tried not to ask too many obvious questions. I found myself craning my neck to see it, trying not to lose sight of that reassuring glint of silver emptying its belly with each wave.

Melkey's women sat together too. Between them they had had twenty children for Melkey. These children, depending on their ages, inclinations and dispositions towards their deceased father, either ran around oblivious, sulked at their mothers' distraction or looked as if they did not wish to be there. Madonna wore her red shoes.

Enen passed us without a word on her way upstairs, stripping herself of her mourning gear and leaving a train of black pieces of skin to the surprised stares of those of us who seemed more comfortable staying in it. It was when she removed her dress that we saw her rounded belly, bursting with emotion behind the waist of her black panties.

"She is mad," said the fishmonger.

"She loved too hard," said the laundry-girl.

"Melkey would not have wanted this for her," said the shopkeeper.

"Her spirit is leaving her," we Bush women whispered wordlessly, among ourselves.

The uninitiated among the grouping started to leave, discomfited, after Enen's naked display of her grief.

Madonna, whose seniority among the clan was determined by the dubious distinction of having been the only woman Melkey ever made his wife, went to the bathroom near the end of the wake and found Enen under water. It was only the mound of her belly, visible above the surface of the liquid from the doorway, that convinced her that Enen was in the tub at all.

We called the ambulance and watched two white-suited men take one of us to the hospital in a screaming vehicle.

"It could be that she is ill. That she cannot help herself. Like her mother…" said Taja.

We all wondered whether there was a trace of insanity infecting our genes.

"Perhaps," said Dear Bush. "But mostly she is stupid."

ENEN

From since I could remember, I had heard that my mother had died of a broken heart, so death from this cause was not amazing to me. My father went to war and never returned.

So deeply had she loved him that my mother assumed he was dead. There was nothing she knew that would keep them apart had he been alive. She languished in a mental hospital during most of my childhood with pictures of him by her side. To me she was just a silent spectre I visited on Sundays in a room that smelled like aloes. Someone who suffered through my reports on my schoolwork and my presentation of drawings composed, at Dear Aunt's insistence, of a smiling mother and daughter holding balloons and ice cream. Someone to wear good dresses and buy apples and flowers for.

Dear Bush took me and witnessed each presentation I made while she plaited my mother's unruly red hair. She always left it in neat rows of tame red plaits. She always returned to find it open and tangled and angry. Had this not been my mother, had I opened the door by mistake and seen her pale face and flaming mane of hair, I would have been scared out of my wits. Despite her being my mother, I sometimes still was.

At her funeral, my father returned from the war with a new wife and a slant-eyed sister and brother for me.

He did not object when Dear Bush insisted that she be allowed to raise me.

FEMI

On that Friday, I arrived at the house Enen shared with Madonna to find the latter sweeping. She said it was something she did when she was scared. Enen had been wandering before but never for this long.

We tried to trace her steps mentally to all the places Madonna had ever found her and repeatedly checked the bathroom to ensure that she had not finally succeeded in finding Melkey under water. We walked the cane with

97

flashlights and entreaties to her to come out if she could hear us. Without success.

The children were silent and wide-eyed.

And then my hair started to curl again.

The other Bush woman was already dead.

ENEN

Melkey called me loudly and often from beyond the grave. I heard him in my sleep. In my dreams we were together and I awoke many times in shock to see that he had disappeared mid-sentence, mid-thought, mid-action. When I went out, I saw his face among crowds. I would start to run behind him until I reached him and found it was somebody else. I seemed closest to him when I was walking the cane.

"Why," I would ask him, among the arrows, "did you leave me this way?"

He had no answers to anything; he just said my name.

When I emerged from the cane, or when I heard Melkey calling me from the water at home, Madonna would be distraught when she came to fetch me. Often she would hide me from the children, placating their queries with explanations of my needing to rest or already being asleep. There were five children then, all boys, so she had a hard time.

Inside, she would approach me with a cloth and some antiseptic water, but since I would already be in the tub, she would often just throw it in the water with me. She would warn me first, but it did not matter; I did not feel the sting of healing.

One time, as she watched the blood run off the cane-blade cuts, she cried. This was after she had been tending to me for a while.

"Why, Enen," she said, "why do you do this to yourself?"

I had looked at her in surprise. I had done nothing. The cane had cut me because I was running through it so fast, so unconscious of its bite, so intent on finding Melkey behind his voice.

"You are dying slowly before my very eyes," she said, "and I do not know what to do about it."

"I am already dead," I told her, truthfully.

"You cannot leave your children," she said.

To that I had said nothing.

Melkey had loved children. He had once told me that it was the duty of every man to make many. This was not always possible with only one woman.

Nevertheless, I tried my best.

"Melkey," I would say when we did it, "we've made another baby."

For days afterwards he would be smiling, treating me gently and attentively, staying indoors to hug and kiss me and help me with the other children. But increasingly, as the number of children increased, the novelty of a new pregnancy decreased and soon he was not attentive at all. He just smiled. When the fishmonger got pregnant, I was also pregnant at the same time. She gave birth to a girl. I to another boy. Melkey was not at home for several days, including the day of the birth. It was Madonna who helped me and was attentive to the baby. She had no choice. Otherwise it would just rouse her from her sleep every night and keep her awake until I managed to still it. It became apparent that she started to like it. After that baby, she destroyed the wall that divided our house and the children ran freely into her quarters from ours. Soon she became like a mother to them, especially the younger ones.

When Melkey came home, seven days after that baby, he said, "But, Enen, it is my first girl-child, and the fishmonger has never had any before," like he expected me to understand.

Once I found out there was another child my death was complete. Without Melkey there did not seem to be a reason for life.

I was just waiting to bring her. I decided to give her that much because she had a part of Melkey and she might be a comfort to the others, who knew I was dead anyway. My only worry was that she would be affected by being housed in such a spiritless place as my body.

On the appointed night I kissed my sons goodbye, although they did not know it then. I thought of kissing Madonna, for all her help, but I knew she would try to stop me. She would have the gift of a family.

I started to walk. I walked so fast I fairly flew and I was no longer aware that my legs were moving. I flew over everything and everyone. Melkey was calling me from the canes again. I did not land until I felt the first pain and even then it took a while for me to come down. I wanted the business to be over quickly so I could fly again to find him.

She came out in the field, in full view of the moon, slipping into the world easily. I looked into her face and at her wet hair. Even at birth you can tell a Bush woman. One of the tribe. And suddenly, there was Melkey, just as strong and as beautiful as the day he left me. I had found him in the cane where he stood without his cutlass or broad hat or boots or profusion of clothing to protect him from the sun and the cane. I called out to him and he nodded. Now I could hear him as plain as day, although it did not seem as if his lips were moving.

"You have been hiding from me," I said to him.

"Never," he said sadly.

"I cannot live without you," I noted.

"To love is to die," said Melkey.

"I am ready," I said.

"You are," he confirmed. We both looked back at the little Bush woman.

"I knew it would be a girl," said Melkey. "Even before you told me."

"Are you worried about them?" I asked

"No," Melkey replied. "They are resilient. And they have Madonna."

"I cannot wait to fly with you," I said to Melkey.

"Well, come on then," said Melkey and we held hands and prepared to fly together.

FEMI

We found the little Bush woman in the cane-field behind Melkey's house where Enen would often retreat to walk the cane. The baby was whimpering next to the body of her mother. Madonna and I were amazed that she was there, unscathed by the blades that surrounded her. We were sure we had looked in that very spot only moments before Dear Bush led us to her. We had seen her tramping through the cane on one of our searches and she said the hair told her the place. We wrapped the child in a cloth and took her back to the house and called the ambulance for Enen, although we knew it was too late. When it came we watched it take her away.

At Dear Bush's house on the Friday before Enen's funeral we all shaved our hair and we put it into a big pile from which Dear Bush wove a wig for Enen. She lay in her casket with our red, red hair fanning her ebony face. She appeared to be sleeping. The Bush women wore veils under which our naked scalps itched. Only the baby retained her hair and she laughed as she played with it on Dear Bush's lap. We gave her an ancient name that meant "In a while".

ENEN

At the end of every thing there is understanding.
No horror, no hope, no pleasure, no pain.
Just knowledge.
Just love.

2. AWAYS

BLIND

Didn't know I was invisible until I passed 106th and Bethel. Must have been. Invisible I mean. Walking along with my mother and she was spitting mean. And rushing me too. Which really pissed me off because I was sweating all over my catsuit and in parts I looked like I was bleeding. My mother was tripping on about me being suspended and all. "Don't think you going spend the day running about with boys and doing *God only knows*… What you need is some good West Indian discipline… Bring you here for some opportunity and you don't even appreciate it…"

Don't know why she bothered to bring me here in the first place. It's cold as ass in the winter. Hotter than chili peppers in the summer and a host of windy, rainy in-betweens. I got suspended for giving it good to Sasha-Marie up in the hallway at the high school. Just only managed to secure me a man after a whole three months and she come batting her breasts in his face trying to take him. Back home, all the girls know beforehand not to mess with me. So I never have to show nobody. Not my fault she brought me here.

Stuck me up in two little rooms over a corner store owned by this yellow Indian lady with a bullseye in the middle of her forehead and rolls of belly coming out of the sides of her sari – Mrs. Laskhmi. Mrs. Laskhmi keep bringing us curry this, curry that on account of my mother having to feed me *and* work the double shift at the doctor's.

Seem like she just be waiting behind her door for Miss Marie to come out for the evening shift to appear with her bowls full of curry. Nasty yellow stuff in Tupperware bowls she always reminding us to bring back. And Miss Marie – she keep taking the bowls and smiling ever so grateful, saying the last curry whatever was oh so good and she will just put it back inside so I can warm it up before she has to hurry off. And then she shutting the door and throwing the stuff right in the bin. And I have to be the one to return Mrs. Laskhmi's stupid Tupperware. Well one day when she came, when Miss Marie had the day *and* the evening shift, I just sat me down and ate me that whole bowl of curry. I almost made myself sick with laughter thinking how Miss Marie's face would look if she had seen me eating that curry. I washed the bowl before she even had to ask me. And I still laugh sometimes thinking that I ate it and she didn't know.

But anyhow, the point is that I had to show Sasha how we do it in St. Kitts. I think I made her swallow a good few of her teeth. Now she bound to think twice before she go messing with my man again. But now I'm suspended and Miss Marie having fits like something terrible. She near wring the bejesus out of my shoulder when the Principal called her. Turns out that she had lost her job the same day. Seems the Doctor got too fresh for her. If she'd a let me, I would have fixed him proper, doctor or no.

Anyways, so Miss Marie been sniffing a job all this week, and all this week I been having to walk up and down, rain, sleet and snow, while she knock on doors begging for work. She says that seeing how it is in the real world will keep my behind in school and on the straight and narrow. Well, I plan to show her. Says if that don't do it, she will send me back to St. Kitts just as fast as day becomes night. I wouldn't mind no how. Except for Roger Sparrow.

Which brings me back to being invisible. 106th and Bethel. Pulling a wedgie out and trying not to walk too close to Miss

Marie, who puffing for a ten o'clock interview and wringing my shoulder something terrible. And there he was: Roger Sparrow coming out of the McDonald's with Ms. Swollen-jaw Sasha. And I'm thinking, "Ain't I done told that bitch?" And Miss Marie stopping at the bus stop – and Roger Sparrow, he looking right at me. Through me. Like I never even there. Even with my red spandex on and a three-inch black belt sharing my waist, in case he missed it in all the red.

Miss Marie done banned me from speaking to Roger Sparrow or Sasha-Marie ever again. But he looking right at me like he wouldn't hear me even if I spoke to him. And then Ms. Sasha was showing him something on her jaw and God bless Marie, he kissed it for her. And I knew I had to be invisible, 'cause the thrashing I gave that girl, she would have to be blind, deaf and dumb to kiss my man right in front of my face like that.

Then the bus pulled up and Miss Marie was yanking my shoulder again and my red wig was almost falling off. So I righted it. And 'fore I could say "God bless Moses" the bus moving on and Roger and Sasha were strolling away. Arm in arm, just as comfy as could be. All I'm thinking is I must be invisible. I said, "Miss Marie, can you see me?" Then I was sorry, because her face, under her best black hat with the yellow rosebuds, looked worse than the last hurricane that hit home two years back. "Don't you be trying no stupidness wid me, gal. I will fix your ass proper. Ain't tekking no foolishness from you."

Long time now I been thinking of running. I was fixing to run with Roger, but now I'm thinking: how can you run with someone who don't even see you? I was fixing to run with Roger because he was my man. Down under the bleachers after school these past two months he been showing me just how much man he was. And I let him. I used to make him sing to me while he did it. The manly part I wasn't too fussy about but, for an American boy, Roger could sing him some

Bob Marley. Last Thursday it was "Waiting in Vain". And for a whole week last term it was "Buffalo Soldier". Just filling me up with all those songs. His notes stroking my ears, closing my eyelids, heavy on my thighs. With those notes Robert don't have to kiss me or even hold me. Mostly he just kept his hands on the bleachers. For balance.

Anyway, that was why I chose him. For his songs. I had imagined him singing to me. All the way out of school gate one in winter, when I'd had my fill of this godforsaken place. All the way down the avenue. All the way onto the bus. All the way to the bus station. Song after song. All the way to the airport, onto the plane. Back to St. Kitts. Now I can't stand to hear another Bob Marley song again. But that Sasha. God bless Moses if I don't get back in that school and fix her proper, and if she ever try to come in my face she going to have to swallow the few teeth I left her with.

"You can't even dress decent to come out," says Miss Marie. We getting off the bus. She on my shoulder as usual. I would never tell Miss Marie about Roger. She don't understand no songs that ain't church songs. And I guess it would be a sin for a man to sing those to her.

Another Indian lady answer the door. Miss Marie say she is here about the baby-sitter position. The woman, she nod. But she don't open the door and she looking at me. I am fixing to tell her why she looking. Miss Marie say, "My relative from the island." And that just throw me 'cause, God bless Moses, I ain't no relative. I am her daughter. Even though I hate her. Even though I told Marie Herschelle that we just friends. Even though I told Roger my mother was dead. I am her daughter.

But Miss Marie, she still talking – "…sick and didn't want to leave her at home. Plus she learning to get around for when she going to school." The Indian woman, she taking in my red catsuit and broad belt and my red boots with the baby-doll heels and the little daisies cut out in them. And my leg-warmers and my denim jacket with the peace patches and my three-inch earrings – red – and my lipstick and my red wig that cost me $19.19 – which back home, by the time they add the tax and everything, would be a fortune. Back home I couldn't afford this hair. But with an allowance from Mr. Roger, I could.

Well, I just take the woman in back. Old coolie chick. No spine left in her. Looking at me with her beady black eyes. Her greasy hair almost cover her face. Her hand taking the keys out the pocket of her housedress. It have pink ribbons round the pockets. Miss Marie, she sit down after she take off her shoes and I just sit down. The apartment dark. It have heavy red curtains with gold thread. It have pictures of people with jade for eyes and six and seven hands and feet sitting cross-legged on the backs of elephants. It dark and red. The chairs red, big and deep. The carpet like blood running under Mrs. Karnani bare yellow feet. It have plastic cover over everything.

The Indian woman say, "Come Phagwan, come Phagwan." And Phagwan come out in the front room, still in his pyjamas, holding a blanket and sucking it and looking at my red wig with his mother's beady black eyes.

"It hard," she saying to Miss Marie, "running the household and caring for Phagwan. We have three other children."

And Miss Marie saying, "Oh me dear, yes, I can understand. It difficult, yes?" And the Indian woman watching Phagwan watch me.

"You have experience?" Miss Marie hand her all the papers that she keep in her purse. References. Health certificate.

"No green card?"

Miss Marie barely shake her head. "Just a few years I here now. It not straighten out yet. But I work real hard!"

The woman ain't saying nothing. Phagwan still swallowing up my hair with black beady eyes.

"Phagwan. Show the nice lady your hamster."

Phagwan race back in the doorway that bring him and come back out with a little rat. Miss Marie never like rats. Miss Marie fidgeting and the woman watching her. Phagwan approach with the thing he holding fast by the scruff of its neck.

He put it on Miss Marie lap and I see her swallow.

"Good little hamster, you take good care of him, Phagwan?" Her hand trembling and it still on her lap. It never even trying to reach the hamster.

There was the time back home when I thought I saw a rat in the kitchen and I shout "Rat!" and almost make Miss Marie burn the bake, she scream and run so hard and fast. That time Miss Marie beat me around the house. And God bless Moses, I swear she almost kill me.

Now Miss Marie just trembling, looking at Phagwan's rat.

"Okay, " say Mrs. Karnani. "Take him back, Phagwan."

Phagwan retreat and return with the blanket.

"There were so many applicants," the woman say, putting on her spectacles to read Miss Marie papers, "So many good people."

"I been doing this forever," say Miss Marie. "I love children. That's the best qualification. When you really love children."

And she motioning to Phagwan to come, come sit on her lap while she talk to his mammy. Phagwan not coming.

"In and out of the house every hour since I put the ad in."

"All I do since I come here is care for children," say Miss Marie, "and at home I took courses in it."

She produce the papers and Mrs. Karnani put them on a side table, a stone elephant that holding up her tea.

It was the last place Miss Marie call before the phone got cut off. Things been hard since the doctors. Which is why I told her she could have left me at home anyways. Can't call nobody nohow.

"So many good people," say Mrs. Karnani.

Phagwan make up his mind and come and sit on Miss Marie. Miss Marie still her hands enough to hug him. Close enough for Mrs. Karnani to see she mean it, but not too close like she could give him any cold she bring with her from outside. She bounce him on her knee and her hat with the yellow rose drop off and onto Phagwan head. He laugh and show her his missing front teeth. And Mrs. Karnani laugh.

Me? I was invisible again.

Miss Marie watch Phagwan turn the hat in his hand.

The hat she keep under her bed in the blue box with the white tissue and the rose petals. She watch Phagwan spin it on his forefinger, watching the flower go dizzy and shed its petals. Miss Marie watch them go flying over Mrs. Karnani's head and land on the papers, catch on the stone eye of the elephant table, the floor. Phagwan laughing. Laughing. Laughing. Smiling with Miss Marie. But is not the Miss Marie I know, 'cause nobody can play with Miss Marie's hats. Far less mash up her flowers.

"Oh, Phagwan," say Mrs. Karnani.

"Is alright," say Miss Marie. "He just a little child. I know how they go. I been caring for them for years."

And just so Mrs. Karnani make up her mind.

Now she talking money. Quiet-like. She understand about the green card. Saturdays too, 'cause is then she do the shopping.

And I crying because I know I loss my skin. My hands, my head. Even in red I can't be seen. Not by Robert and not by my mother.

At the bottom of the stoop of Mrs. Karnani's building, after she has retrieved her petals and put on her shoes and rustled Phagwan's rat-like hair, Miss Marie try to grab up my shoulder.

But I raise my fist to her and twist away and I dare her to

try and touch me. She frown at me. She shake her head. She start to walk. Talking about if I was back home in the island and which tamarind rod she would keep for me.

But I don't mind her. She not going trouble me again. Don't see why I was ever afraid of her in the first damn place. Is now I see she is just another woman. And God Bless Moses, is as woman she have to see me.

THE UNDOING

When I come home my mother is watching television. Cheetahs running after a giraffe. She is wearing lipstick and a bra the same pink as her rollers. The rollers she will remove a few minutes before he comes in and then she will tease her hair with a rat-tail comb and put on perfume. Before I went away to camp she used to pull the hairs out of the middle of her head. Now, in the after-camp, she uses a comb to coax the rest of the hair over the bald spot.

My mother is also wearing boots. And beans. The boots she's had forever. Relics of her hippie days. They are vinyl – hi-polish. They have pretty iridescent stars in them and are pink also, but darker. The beans would be new. The colours I cannot tell because they are beneath the right cup of the bra. Harry brings them home from work for her and pretends he does not know what she does with them. At breakfast sometimes he says, "Gotta get you some beans, girl, you gotta be careful – eating so many beans will make you fat." And my mother laughs – a frail and coughy laugh that makes the round edges of the sweets bump against each other and create little bulges where a breast should be.

She has been here all day, watching the carnage. The cheetah catches the giraffe and tears into it. My mother does not flinch.

"Wanna know what Jane did today?" I ask her.

"What?" she says from far away. My mother is not a freak or anything. She answers me when I say something.

"The new girl – she cut herself in art class with the stencil knife and another girl fainted."

"Oh," says my mother.

"And they sent Jane to the school nurse and she told Jane that she needs to see the psychologist because she's sure Jane cut herself on purpose and people that cut themselves on purpose are ill in the head… But Jane told them it was an accident."

"Did she?" says my mother, watching vultures hover over the giraffe's remains.

When Harry gets up from sleeping he goes to mow the lawn. He gets up at four in the morning to do it. I'm not sure whether it's because that is the time he feels the garden needs to be made right or whether he wants to give my mother a reason why he has not been next to her in bed at that hour. She does not ask him for any. When he is finished he sets fire to the bundles he has raked up and watches them crackle, smoke and spit. From the window I watch him take off his shirt even though it is cold and the tyres around his belly jiggle as he pushes up and down and the motor drones. The mower coughs up bits of grass.

The school psychologist says there are things to be thankful for in every situation. I am thinking, well, what could I be thankful for about Harry, but I figure that if there was no Harry I wouldn't know what cut grass smells like at four o' clock in the morning. Jiggle. Drone. Jiggle. Drone. The mower is not unlike the psychologist's voice. He is a tiny man and always looks tired.

When I go downstairs my mother is already there in her make-up. She is cooking Harry's bacon and watching "Discovery". Mating tarantulas. My mother is riveted. She is occasionally putting a hand in her bra and eating the beans one by one. They pass her teeth in rhythm. One two three. Stop. Four. Stop. One two three... I can see their colours now. When Harry is finishing she will excuse herself to top them back up again. She tops them up in private.

She sees that I am dressed for school and kisses me goodbye in the kitchen. She does not go outside because the heat melts jellybeans and makes them all sticky. It could be a mess. If she is, say, at the grocery and the front of her dress starts to bleed rainbows, well, people might think her crazy or something.

"Nobody at school wants to talk to Jane. Well, except me," I tell my mother.

"Really," says my mother. Pink. Blue. Green. Stop.

"They don't want to talk to her since she threw herself down the stairs. It was right after the notices in assembly. Jane ran up to the podium and opened her mouth and started to scream, then closed it and threw herself down the steps to the stage."

Red. Stop.

"Was she hurt?" says my mother. She is just like any other normal mother, concerned at the possibility of injury to a child.

"Minor lacerations. The psychologist says that she did it to get attention and that Jane is a very disturbed little girl."

My mother almost trips over herself when the mower stops, trying to have her beans in place and Harry's bacon on the plates before his boots hit the welcome mat.

The spiders stop mating. One of them is about to kill the other.

"I told her to get help," I say, helpfully.

The summer I came home from camp and walked through the door and saw Harry and my mother in her stuffed

115

underwear, I did not say hello. Instead, Harry said. "Your mother lost her breast." He said it by way of explanation for why he was still there, even after she had called the cops on him. He said it like she had been, say, out playing tag with some friends and then she had to leave and when she got home she realized her breast was missing. He said it like, say, if she was real, real, careful, she could retrace her steps and maybe find it.

My mother had promised that he would be gone after camp. Which is why I went in the first place. Which is why I agreed to a new school after camp. But Harry stayed and took my mother to dress her scar and fed her soup after her radiation treatments and sat with her while she was crying. I could see my mother needed to have him back. Which is why I didn't hold her to all her promises.

Sometimes he held her close to his chest and nuzzled her bald spot. And sometimes I watched and wondered whether he could feel her hard little beans through her dress. And sometimes when he saw me staring at them together he said to me to go outside and play.

But no one wanted to play with me.

I asked the school psychologist, "Do you think maybe people can change?" and he thought it was a sign of improvement – one of those positive indicators he wrote about in my file that meant I was on my way to recovery – the turning point when I realized that my life was in my own hands and I needed to take account of myself. He had never had such a wicked new student. So he puffed up (naturally) and he said, "Of course they can, if they really want to." And I said, "Even child-abusers? And men who sleep with their girl-friend's daughters at night? Men who whip them with belts when they did something wrong and lick the welts off later? Can those people change?" And the psychologists turns colours like my mother's jellybeans and he says, "Those people, maybe not." And I say, "Well, what is the sense in those people living if they can't change? Wouldn't it be better if somebody just killed them?" And he is silent a while and then he says, "Perhaps." And I say, "That's all I wanted to know." And he says, "Come here, Jane," but I am already running.

Suppose, say, you were up on the roof one day and your mother was below you in the kitchen eating beans out of her bra and her boyfriend was at work and you were supposed to be at school and you weren't and your mother was so deep in "Discovery" (Praying Mantis) that she did not think that the noise above was not the pigeons. And suppose you were thinking of endings like the psychologist said (happy ending based on logical but optimistic reasoning) and suppose you could see your teacher from school pull up in a car with the psychologist and some policemen behind them. I wanted to ask him, "Wouldn't you want to become a bird and fly away from it all?" Because birds are free. And birds do not think of endings when they spread their wings to escape the sound of sirens.

FUTURE IMPERFECT

When I was a girl I christened my unborn children with names I wrote in cursive in the backs of diaries, old exercise books and scraps of paper. Names like Alexandria Danielle. Lydia Mercedes. Aryanna Michaela. I did not write surnames because I took for granted a husband whose tribe I could not have foreseen. Surnames were not yet the important business. I did not write boys' names because the thought of giving birth to those whose presence, at the time, I found particularly abhorrent was unthinkable. I was a long way off fantasizing about the boys on television, appending their last names to my first and trying the combinations on my tongue.

I wrote the names and hid the books in secret places so I could refer to them when the time came.

My son is on his haunches, examining something on the floor. His hands are folded across his open lap. His eyes are wide as he ponders this object. I see the wrinkled carcass of a pea. Or perhaps a dried and atrophied piece of leaf. My son. He sees a gold nugget he has just discovered at the bottom of a stream. He sees the undiscovered fossil of a past era. He sees a piece of Popeye's power-giving spinach. Or Superman's kryptonite. Which he promptly eats. And he grimaces because what he has eaten does not taste like it.

My son and I are waiting.

Three hours ago I bathed him in bubbles that he caught in his hands and threw in the air and burst with the breath of his laughter. Two hours ago I washed his soft hair and combed it. Minutes later I oiled his skin and dressed him in his best pants. The ones he detests. I spared him the rest of his clothing while I starched and ironed one of the shirts his father bought him. It has a Hawaiian print that we both hate. All the while he was flying an aeroplane. His arms were wings that dipped and swerved and finally allowed him to crash on the carpet. Which is when he discovered the Kryptonite he just ate.

"Why," he asks me, "do I have to dress up to see him?"

"Sometimes," I tell him, as we negotiate the shirt, "you have to show people how beautiful, how special you are. Some people cannot see those things unless their eyes are first trapped by how good you look on the outside."

"Even your own family?" asks my son.

"Even your own family," I reply.

"Even your own father?" he wonders.

"Even your own father," I reply and I kiss the top of his head.

"Even you?" he asks and the fear in his eyes makes him seem wise.

"Never, never me," I say.

My son. He understands because he is careful not to soil his pants while we are waiting. He does not roll and writhe on the carpet as he tries to cross the enemy lines he has demarcated in its green undergrowth. He mimics the sound of gunfire in a moderate tone. He walks instead of runs from the offensive, but cannot escape within such restrained parameters. Without that capacity, trying to escape is pointless and he is forced to abandon the game.

In the beginning his father walked straight lines on the hospital linoleum and smoked cigarettes while he waited for me to assist his son with making an appearance. He brought his car around to the exit a few days later and let the engine idle while the nurse wheeled us downstairs. At my house he made several bottles of formula he measured carefully, levelling each scoop of powder with the blade of a sterilized knife, and stored them in the refrigerator in anticipation of an appetite befitting his offspring. He drew baths for me and offered to hold the son he named Ansari while I rested in the steam. I had not prepared any boy names. By the time boys became less objectionable, the name-writing game had lost its charms.

Ansari is looking through the window. His breath is making little clouds on the glass that he wipes off with his hands and then makes over again. He is fidgeting from foot to foot, resting his weight on the outer edges of his new black sneakers, which he has not yet bent into the shape of his feet. His nose is pressed against the glass and he is counting the red cars that pass our apartment, trying to guess which number will herald the arrival of his father. I have placed a little blue knapsack by the door that he eyes indifferently. It may mean nothing at all today. It didn't last week but it did the Sunday before that when, from all accounts, he had a wonderful time. On his last birthday we waited until nine, with him on my lap, and then we took the knapsack inside and emptied it onto his bed and I allowed him to wear his new Spiderman pyjamas – the ones that we had been saving for special occasions. Like when he goes to visit his father. That time the pyjamas did not stop his tears. He cried in my arms and it was impossible to read him a story. So I curled up and held him against my belly in the curve made by my chest and legs. And we waited for the next time.

Today it is past three without a sign and the cars, so far, have numbered one hundred and forty-eight.

On my son's third birthday we had a party at my

apartment for just the three of us. While I cut the birthday cake on the kitchen counter, my son and his father sat on the carpet examining a large dump-truck in bright colours that he had bought. Their heads were pressed close together as the older pointed out to the younger what parts fitted where. I remember thinking to myself: this is as it should be – although I was not sure whether I meant the father being with the son or him being there with both of us. That time his father left at two in the morning, after he had put Ansari to bed and spent a few hours snoozing beside him with Ansari's little hand holding his tightly. It was the latest he had ever stayed with us – before or since.

When Ansari was born it was just after two in the afternoon – working hours – and so, the father had joked, he had not been obliged to come up with a story for the Parrot. The Parrot is what he calls his wife. She strikes me as a nervous woman – although I have never seen or spoken to her. I do not know her given names, whether she works, how she dresses. I imagine her covered in bright feathers, confined to a beautiful house, repeating in her husband's voice the excuses he gives her after he has been with me.

I first met the father when I was selling him some ceramic whistling frogs.

"My wife," he had confided, "loves exotic things."

"Oh," I had said, as I wrapped them in the *New York Times* so that they would not break in the jostle and grind of his briefcase. "Really? Like what?"

"Anything, really," he had said. "Animals you do not see except at the zoo. Clothing that is handwoven by tribal women in Africa or India. Pots that are painted with dyes someone has had to crush seasonal berries to make."

I took my first look at him then to see if he was serious. And we both laughed.

"Sorry," I said. "These frogs were made right here in the back of the shop. By me."

"I think that will be our little secret," he said. "She'd be disappointed."

I remember folding the creased paper over the back of the frog, its open-mouthed amazement frozen in time as I covered its head with yesterday's news. He had been my last customer for the day and I was looking forward to closing the door behind him and retreating to a gaggle of geese I had started to fashion from papier-mâché.

"She would like you," he said when I handed him the package with his change.

"I beg your pardon?"

"You're exotic," he said. "Your skin is the colour of egg-plant. Your hair is coarse, yet it tumbles down your back. You look like you come from a place where people make paint from crushed berries. You could probably tell her about things she has never seen before."

I laughed at him.

"I was born and bred here," I said. "Your wife probably knows more about crushing berries than I do."

It was the first and last time we ever spoke in any detail about the Parrot.

After our first date I decided that Suda was a bust. There was nothing I had done that he had not done sooner, nothing that I saw that he had not already seen. No place I'd gone to that was further, stranger, colder, higher than somewhere he had been before. Still, I let him continue to visit, even after our dates became limited to him coming to my house to lie in bed with me, stroke my egg-plant skin and trap his hands in my hair.

And suddenly there was Ansari.

Then there were no more late nights caressing each other's differences.

When I was a girl, I disc-jockeyed my wedding on pristine sheets of white foolscap paper, printing the names of the songs and artists in order of play. I put asterisks beside the titles of the songs I liked the best (the lyrics of which were never long enough on the radio) to be re-mixed and re-peated at various stages of the party. No. 1 was "At Last" by Etta James – First Dance: Bride and Groom – down to No. 12, "Sexual Healing" by Marvin Gaye – Removal of the Garter Belt. My face had felt hot when I wrote that one, though I put three dots in place of the first three letters of the song's title lest my mother find it. I hid this list in a box at the top of my wardrobe, beneath such innocuous articles as my Enid Blyton collection and my Barbie doll-house. I hid them lest my mother think me presumptuous in thinking of such womanly business as marriage. I hid the list between the glossy pages of magazines with dress-designs I found wedding-worthy, bound together by pieces of satin ribbon, stained with the scent of dried roses.

"You couldn't call?" I ask him the following day in the park, where he agreed to meet me. He is late, and when he arrives he is careful not to exchange our customary brush of lips on each cheek. Instead, he brings his hand to rest on my shoulder, like a big brother assisting me with a small difficulty I have told him about in the middle of a shopping expedition in his area. Only we could not be brother and sister. We look nothing alike.

"I was scheduled to go to a function after seeing the boy and I ran late. The Parrot was rushing me. There just wasn't time."

It occurs to me that someone passing could think him odd. Could mistake his reference to be about a bird.

"Ansari reached 203 red cars," I tell him. "It got so dark he could no longer get the colours right. He begged me to turn on the outside lights. He cried. And then he fell asleep."

Suda's face is blank. He's looking at me as if I am speaking to him in a language he cannot understand.

"What would you like me to do?" he asks. "Should I send him something later?"

"Once upon a time," I observe, "you could have brought it with you when you came to see me."

He is vaguely embarrassed, as if I am referring to a stage of his life of which he is not proud. He looks around furtively at passers-by: the woman with the twins in a stroller, taking a brisk walk for exercise; the two old men playing at chess, but really making conversation out of memories; the young lovers kissing at the edge of the fountain, oblivious of the sprays of water, the breeze of bird wings, the despair of two people.

"Look, I said I'm sorry."

I am walking away from him and my eyes smart from the sting of goodbye. He does not even try to stop me.

The first time that my son went to the Parrot house he was five years old. I do not know if Suda had told her about him before then, only that one day he called and said to get Ansari ready, he would be around to pick him up. I asked him what I should pack, where were they going, and he said he was taking my son to meet his wife.

I sat on my sofa for most of the day and watched the clock.

When my son came home and I asked him how his day was, he was full of stories about a playroom with oversized stuffed animals and baby-sized furniture and a video and tapes lined up just waiting for him to watch, and a puppy they named Puppy. He was not so good at describing the Parrot.

"How does she look?" I asked him.

"Like a mommy," he said, although we both knew she had no children.

"Is she fun?" I asked.

"She's alright," he said, and then he went back to telling me about the animals again.

I consider visiting the Parrot. Turning up at her cage and having her repeat after me my name, the date I met Suda, the syrupy logic of his excuses to her for the many hours we spent together, the name of my son, his age, the similarities between himself and his father. I imagine her stupefied face on top of her layers and layers of bright clothing.

Then I decide that it does not matter what she looks like in reality or whether her moniker is justified.

Today we are not waiting for Suda, although he has promised to come to take our son to a kiddie restaurant for his birthday. My son. He is sitting on his new Spiderman sofa, painting his mouth and fingers in the birthday cake we bought. His hair has been washed for his birthday but I have not combed it since he returned from roughhousing with the neighbour's nephew. He is wearing his favourite swim-trunks and his well-worn Pokemon t-shirt. He is bare-footed. He is laughing.

"Ansari," I call, and he looks at me with his father's dark eyes, his manner of looking at the world from the very roots of his thick eyelashes. My family's long fingers brush away Suda's thick, wiry hair. The only thing that is peculiarly my son's and no one else's is perhaps his ignorance of his tribe and his ignorance of the fact that he does the things he does because several men did them just that way for generations before him. This is not something that he will not learn *because* Suda does not live with us, although it is easier for a child who sees it every day. But it will continue to elude him if Suda does not integrate their lives, does not give my son a sense of where he belongs by letting him see the similarity of their make-up.

"You are beautiful," I tell him. "You look like your father."

"Are we going to get dressed up for him, now?" he asks.

"We are not."

"Then how will he see how beautiful I am?" he asks, bewildered.

"If he cannot see it, we cannot show him," I say.

My son. He smiles at me through cake, displaying the split between the front teeth I wore as a child. He is building something out of Lego. It starts as a truck. It becomes a U-haul. It evolves into a skyscraper – the Empire State building – and he into a demolition team. His hand is the big ball that in a single pendulum-swing erases the work of a thousand hours. The world comes crashing down while he rolls in it. He laughs at it. The death of the establishment merely means a chance to rebuild.

When I was a girl I gave my unborn children names I wrote in coloured inks in the backs of my diaries, in old exercise books, on scraps of paper. Names like Richelle Alexis. Christy Susanne. Rosalinda Delarosa. I did not write surnames because I took for granted a husband whose lineage I had not foreseen. It did not occur to me then that the children's surnames could be my own. Or that they might be boys. That a husband might never come. Or that the father of my son could be married and painfully absent from our lives.

That was not the way I had imagined it.

THE DOLL

When we parted he went up the escalator on the way to his plane and I stood at the bottom, twisting the doll around and around in my hands while I watched the steps ascend and disappear into oblivion. He did not look back and this, more than even the doll, disturbed me. There was no parting glance, no reluctance etched on his face. He offered a quick perfunctory kiss, looked at his watch and stepped on board the travelling staircase in response to a polite last boarding call. It was not my fault that he was last. He had not made a mental note of his flight number, thought he was due to catch a later flight and therefore ignored all the previous calls until they called him by name. It was the reason he would not be able to meet Jane.

We had not been doing anything special. He had been sitting next to me in the departure lounge, reading a newspaper I had bought for him from a nearby shop. I had got up to stretch my legs, make myself useful and break the silence that enveloped us. I knew that he was not really reading the page when I asked him what he thought about some star's miscarriage and he said "What?" like he did not know what I was talking about, even though his eyes had seemed glued to the story for the past fifteen minutes.

"She lost her baby," I said and pointed at the unnaturally slim woman with amazingly long and lustrous hair. I did not try to hide the fact that I was not sorry. I was not glad. But I wanted him to agree that no life was perfect. It was just that some imperfections were more visible than others. I wanted him to think that there were some advantages to loving a woman with average looks, above average weight and nice-enough hair. I wanted him to understand that there were some people who would choose to stay with such a woman. A woman with an alright job in an OK company. I wanted him to acknowledge that a life with such a woman had its benefits – like the ability of such a woman to carry children to term. My mother had done it for him once. (But then again, so had Jane – not for him, of course – and she still looked like a star.)

He grunted and stared at the woman again.

"She looks a bit like my wife," he said. He peered at the picture to establish the resemblance.

It was not the first time that he had spoken about her. She had been the spectre haunting our conversation for the three hours he was on stop-over. But for the fact that we had never seen each other before, he and I could have been old friends. I already knew her life-story without ever having been put to the inconvenience of living any part of it with her. He seemed worried about what our meeting (or rather, perhaps, the confirmation of my existence) would mean for his marriage.

I wanted to put his mind at ease by telling him that, had he told her about me, she probably would not have wanted to attend this reunion anyway. It would mean little in her scheme of things. I was already grown and wanted nothing from them but to lay my eyes on him. He could give me that alone. It was the reason I suspected that he had not told her about today. Why upset her over a mistake that happened years ago? But I said nothing.

We had all got on with our lives. At least, he had. And the

way that he referred to her suggested that he hoped that I had too. There was mutual curiosity but there would be no lasting complications. There was no reason to involve her.

But he had never before said she was so beautiful.

We went back to our respective silences and I thought about Jane. I wondered whether she would ever describe me as beautiful to another person in just that way. Unlikely. I knew her to be truthful to the point of being brutal.

In one of our silences he had handed me a present. Previously he had held it in the crook of his arm, a slim white box to which my eyes invariably wandered. He had stretched it out to me and I had been excited, not because we had any tradition of gift-giving, but because I was curious as to what he would give me. Now. After all this time.

A doll. Porcelain. Hand-painted. Immobile eyes of blue glass observing the world in a state of catatonia. Hard, heavy limbs projecting from a body that was stuffed with sponge under a frilly floral dress.

"Thank you," I said quietly, and I held her carefully by the waist, afraid that I might drop and break her.

"They are collector's items, those," he said by way of validation. He had guessed that I did not understand the significance of the gift.

"It's very pretty."

He had nodded and returned to his paper and silence.

Several women passed us in the airport lounge, giving him appreciative glances and wondering what my connection to him could possibly be. He sat with his knees apart on a backless bench, stylishly rumpled in a crisp white shirt with French cuffs, tight faded jeans, black leather boots. A black leather jacket lay beside him. He carried no other luggage but his guitar case and a black leather backpack. His hair had been cut and dyed by a stylist, his nails were salon-buffed. He did not look like my father. He did not look like anybody's father.

"This is Jane," I said, as I removed Jane's likeness from my wallet. His eyes brightened as every man's did when I introduced or referred to Jane or her likeness. Jane is a looker. She has one son who is similarly gorgeous, from a man who is not present other than financially, and so does not complicate their lives, and one pretty daughter from a fleeting union right before she met me. She has never told her daughter's father that she exists.

"Ah," he says, and he looks at me.

"She should be here any minute." Jane runs a shop in the city where she sells her own pottery and art and pieces she collects from all over the world. In our early days I would imagine her crouched over a roll of raw clay, hair tumbling into her eyes, and the image would be inexplicably erotic. I never saw her face or her legs or her breasts in my vision. It would just be her hair. On Fridays, Jane closes the shop late because she gets a lot of customers from the wine bar next door who are tantalized to find her open at ungodly hours of the night, selling Art. This is not the reason she is late. Tonight, Jane has to attendher son's school pantomime. Then she must leave him and his sister with a sitter while she meets a new artist, with whom she wishes to co-exhibit, for dinner and drinks. The exhibition will also include recordings of Jane reading her first book, published to critical acclaim.

Everybody I tell about Jane, to whom I show her picture, asks me what the catch is. What are the traits that are not immediately visible that might make her even a slightly objectionable person. When I say there is nothing much that I can think of – besides the fact that she is so perfect – they nod as if they pity me anyway. One woman at my workplace said, "God, that's so unfair," as if I would immediately comprehend what "that" was and what was unfair about it.

Evidently nothing could be postponed so she could be here for all three hours, though I know she would have tried.

Indeed, Jane will drive several miles here so she can help me say goodbye to my father, after meeting him for the first time in my adult life. She does not consider this a huge undertaking. She is my girlfriend.

"Your girlfriend, the one you told me about…" he is making sure he has not misunderstood me, that this gorgeous creature is truly a lesbian and worse, in love with his ordinary, estranged daughter.

I nod. It is then that we hear the final call. The one with his name in it, threatening, in the most dulcet of tones, to remove his luggage from the plane and leave without him.

"Oh, you won't get to meet her!" I say.

He double checks his ticket and we discover his mistake. He does not apologize. I can tell he is not the type.

My father is a musician. He plays guitar for several famous singers – on the road and in the studio. It is not hard to imagine young girls fainting when he walks on stage, or even throwing him their panties.

He was not difficult to trace when my mother died. His picture and the address of a studio that had produced an album he had worked on were among her things. My mother had been fat and ordinary. Like me. The fact that they had shared something – that was the surprising part. The fact that he failed to turn up for her funeral was to be expected. Nor was his agreeing to spend all three hours of his stop-over with a daughter he met once in infancy and never saw again all that surprising, because he did not look at it as a chance to meet me. He looked at it as a chance to allow me to meet him.

Perfunctory kiss. Hop on elevator. Me holding doll.

Our three-hour meeting is over and we return to our respective lives.

Last night I had tossed and turned in Jane's arms at the prospect of the meeting.

"What are you expecting?" she asked, turning on the light. "Perhaps if we talk about it, it will feel better."

It did not. Partly because I did not know what I was expecting. Instead, it threatened to degenerate into a row. Jane thought that I was looking for some sort of validation or approval from this man. Jane thought that I needed to see it just as an opportunity to put a face to the name that had contributed biologically to my presence on the planet. Nothing more. I could tell that it was the same reasoning she expected to apply to her daughter's queries one day. In the end, she held me while I wept my confusion on her shoulder and comforted me even in my refusal to accept her clarity.

Jane had been similarly supportive when my mother died. She had stood on my right at the graveside while I wept. Provided me with tissues. She had left her children with the sitters for the day so that all her strength could be directed towards me. On our way to the funeral, I had questioned the world from behind tear-blurred shades. Jane said, "Your mother is out of her suffering, Hannah, be thankful for her life and be happy for the end of her pain." Jane does not spend a lot of time crying. About anything. She always says that any tears that do not express joy are useless. It is a credo she lives by.

It did not help.

At the graveside my tears were still copious. The people who came to extend me their condolences found themselves speechless at the sight of my emotional disintegration and ended up talking to Jane instead. She was a vision of composure in a black wrap dress and slingbacks, shadeless and sobre. They asked her who she was to me. Jane said, "A friend." Jane does not ever say "'girlfriend", always "friend". It leads you to think that because friendships are not mutually exclusive, there could be other me's in her life. We have never discussed committment.

Jane comes running, hair deliciously askew, turning heads as she sprints across the car park and into the departure hall.

"Sorry," she looks at her watch, "I ran late."

We kiss. One of those friendly lip-to-cheek affairs. But her face is etched with genuine concern for me. She examines mine for a sign of how it went. I betray nothing. She looks at the doll.

"Wow," she says. "Is that a Bergedoff? These are collector's items."

She is freshly interested in the enigma that is my father. "Where is he?"

I gesture towards the escalator.

"He got the time wrong; he was actually leaving at ten so he had to rush."

She is obviously disappointed and cranes her neck to see if she can yet catch a glimpse of him. I laugh to myself. How would she know who he was even if she did see him? We look nothing alike. You would never place him with me. You might place him with her. People like them belonged together.

"Well, how did it go anyway?"

She is ready to recover from having missed seeing him. It is characteristic of her to move on. Life is short. Time's a-wasting. Things to do and people to see and all that. She is ushering me towards the car park where we will get into her Land Rover and she will drive us back to her place. Several people will call her on her mobile and she will conduct animated conversations with them. She will likely call the sitter, her mother, whom I've never met, and any one of several friends whom I have. I will settle into my leather seat and strap in for the ride and watch how assuredly she manoeuvres the big vehicle at speed to the toll gate where she will halt with a screech. The ticket agent will be a man. He will smile at Jane and ask her if she is having a nice day. She will remind him that it is night time – on her it will

133

be the perfect thing to say. He will think her clever and take his time stamping and returning her receipt, which she will snatch from him and discard in the tray between us before powering out of the gate without a goodnight. I will wonder, as I usually do, how people so unwittingly give people like Jane their hearts without a recommendation. Jane does not suffer fools, or people she does not know, gladly. She often does not suffer people she does know.

"It was OK," I begin. "Whatever it was that I expected, I think it came close."

"Good." She is removing something from her purse. Her cellular. "Now that is out of your system you can live your life again."

"Well, he is a part of my life," I say.

She rolls her eyes. She does not bother to repeat the biological contributor and nothing else speech.

"I thought I'd watch the plane leave," I tell her.

We are almost in the car. She is about to make a call. Probably the sitter.

"Does it really make sense, Hannah?" she says, but she does not press the call button. "Will it change anything?"

"That isn't the point," I reply. "I want to see it fly off."

We watch each other from either side of the big jeep. "Why?"

"I don't think I need a reason to watch my own father leave," I say miserably.

She is hurt.

"I never suggested that you did," she explains patiently, "it's just that the plane has probably already taxied down the runway. You'd be lucky if you saw it anyway."

I start to gather my will to walk back inside and she sees it.

"Well, if you must, I'll go with you."

It is not unlike her to offer.

"No," I say. "You go on ahead. Call the sitter. I'll take the train back."

She is perplexed out of a rebuttal. Opens her mouth to say it is not a problem. But nothing comes out except, "If you say so."

"Do you want me to take it back for you?" she asks rhetorically. "Jeez, it's priceless!" She looks at it with reverence. It is something she would hold carefully in her perfect fingers and admire.

"No," I say. "I want you to have it."

I hand over the doll. She shakes her head. Her body says she feels she cannot take it. It is something that my father gave to me.

"Have her," I say. "I certainly would not know what to do with her. It is something to remember me by."

She starts to laugh, "Hannah, I don't need a doll to. . ."

The awareness that we are breaking up dawns suddenly on her perfect features. In the dark I see her stiffen. The way you do to take a blow. She is trying to back up, to retrace her steps to the landmark she missed. The point that signalled that the trip to the airport would be the end. The sign that said, "This way to break-up." We both missed the sign but we are still here.

"Hannah, it was just a stupid spat about a plane," she reasons, softly.

"It was not a spat. It is not you," I say.

Her tears are the worst kind to the person who has caused them. They fall silently. She does not whimper. She does not talk or spit insults or make any sound at all. She does nothing while she cries but feel pain.

She takes the doll and looks into its glassy eyes as I turn to re-enter the airport.

She must have loved me to cry that way.

THE NEIGHBOURS

They sit close to the ground on a ledge at the bottom of the stairs. Between them they occupy the two flats near the end of the row, closest to the stop for the 36, 121 and 53. Despite this they are generally, and deliberately, un-noticed. A dog lounges somewhere in their midst, tail wagging in slow-motion, half-opening one black eye.

You hear them the moment you step onto the first concrete step that marks the daily descent. You cannot help it. There is the buzz of the motor on the wheelchair of the crippled one when his atrophied right hand grasps a bulbous control and he moves, robotized. Forward. Backward. Over the dog's tail. Yelping. Laughter. "Shit!" This from the one holding the leash who does not know how else to respond to his friend's mirth and the dog's bewildered pain. There is the hollow clink of their beer bottles hitting the concrete to punctuate their exchanges. There is the scratch of a match on concrete, the silence during a light-up, the mumbled comment on the tail-end of a breathless first inhalation. There are four of them, if you don't count the dog. Two of them could be brothers.

"Oy, there's Sandy," says the crippled one. It sounds like "Oy, tears 'andy". His neck cannot support his head. It lolls in the direction of his right shoulder. His chin teeters at a 45 degree angle to his chest. Somebody has covered his hair with an old grey cap, beneath which his grey hair hangs limp.

Sandy does not wish to be seen today. Sandy would very much like to be left alone.

"Handy!" he warbles from his twisted lips, and spittle sprays and sinks into his scarf. He thinks you have not heard him. His friends know that despite his best efforts he could never be missed.

"Sandy! Sandy! Sandy!" They join him in the way you call someone for an encore. The way you encourage someone who has not done it quite right the first time. The way you say, "Come down again, Sandy, and say hello the way you did yesterday. Have a word with us. Ask after the dog", without saying those words at all.

You slam the door. Partly because it is threatening rain again and the freezer section will be extra cold at the off-licence and Mr. Rajesh will have you in there even though he knows full well your coat has no lining, peering at the people on the right side of the freezer shelves, greeting them from behind and between the milk and bacon they are about to buy.

You slam the door because the blasted drunks on the corner by the bus stop will not leave you alone.

You wonder if they heard him come in after four again this morning. Heard his motorcycle slide into its spot, heard him chain it to the iron railing, heard him swear as he tried to find his way up the stairs, heard him curse again as he tried to find the keys and then the keyhole. When he passed your bedroom door you pretended to be asleep. As if you had not been up all night worrying about him.

You slam the door because in between your worrying in the wee hours and this descent, there hasn't been enough space to put on a pretty face.

"Mom," he mumbled this morning when confronted by your apparition. "You are a ghost of yourself at this hour."

"This came for you," you said.

There was another robbery last night. Once upon a time

you used to listen to the crime reports, your heart gripped by something you could not explain, praying he was not a victim. Now you listen to the crime reports praying he is not the criminal.

The envelope was white and clean, like the collars where it came from. He took it in his blunt-blackened hands and slit it with the back end of the breadknife you brought him. You waited. His eyes raced across the lines and then retreated into his head again and were unreadable. He returned to his hangover.

You did not need to read it to know what it said.

So you put on your coat and come down the stairs.

And you slam the door.

"Fuck off!" you say to the crippled one.

His eyes bug open and they all fall silent.

The dog growls half-heartedly from somewhere at the back of his throat.

THE PROMISED LAND

I mean, it ain't that he don't love me. Don't get me wrong
or nothing – alotta things may be wrong with Arlen,
depending on who you listen to, but there ain't no doubt in
my mind that he do love me. So I guess most people would
say, so what the hell you doing here then – and he ain't even
with you.

Boy, if Arlen knew that I ain't really at the nail shop
getting filled. If I wasn't planning on telling him that there
was this wedding party taking forever to get tips, and then
I stopped at Tish's afterwards and we just got lost on the
time that her cousin Cybil crashed her own mother's
wedding. Well, if I wasn't planning on telling him all that,
and I was just gonna tell him the truth, straight up, no chaser,
well, Arlen would likely have a right fit, he would. He would
likely get all bug-eyed and bull-frogged and start breathing
fast or not at all and say, "Woman, are you plain out of your
cotton-picking mind?" Most of our quarrels that start that
way end up in the silent treatment. Days Arlen and I be
quietly trampling along each other's fringes. Not a solitary
sound save the protest of whatever we get too close to. Me
clanging the dishes in the sink; him slapping the remote
against his flank during WWF – though I done told him how

much it annoys me; me dropping an egg I meant to fry him at breakfast and it splattering out on the floor just as sharp as him raking his chair away from the table with his butt and leaving for work without eating. And it'd be like that a good few days. At least until one of us just bumps into the other in the kitchen or one of our hands finds the other's to pass the telephone when one of the children calls and we pretend as if we ain't fighting after all, cause no matter how old they get, children still get jittery to hear their folks is fighting. Or one of us will roll over in bed and find a body that sleep don't know, ain't on speaking terms, and we will stroke it anyway.

That is what would normally happen. But I can't swear on it this time if I told Arlen about this. I can't swear that, after thirty-two years, Arlen wouldn't just take himself and his things up and out of our house for this. Ain't many things I don't know about Arlen after thirty-two years, but this is definitely one of them – which is why I'm here by my own self. Which is why I let Arlen put me off outside the nail shop and drive on down the street while I went inside the nail shop and waited a few moments, like I was catching my breath and deciding whether the crowd might be enough to make me come back another day. It's why I turned around and came back out and walked the three blocks through a bad neighbourhood. It's why all the time I am walking I'm thinking, Lord, please don't let the man turn back to tell me something that couldn't wait, or to return my house keys or my *Daily Word* that I left in the truck, and come and find me hustling up the street in the wrong direction. But I checked all those things was on me and when I got here I called the nail shop to say I was supposed to come over but I got caught up, and ask did my husband pass by to collect me, cause he sometimes pass back to pick me up even though we ain't arranged nothing, or it's earlier than the time cause sometimes he says he was just in the area and he thought maybe he would check and see if I'm done, but I know he just want the company. But the lady in the nail shop says no, he ain't been back there, and for a hot minute I maybe feel a little sad, cause maybe if she had said that he was there, wondering where the hell I was, I would have hightailed it back and run the three blocks and told him the salon was so full when I got there and so hot and high with all the acrylic and everything that I took a walk and then the walk was so good I didn't want to stop and I wasn't gonna bother with the fill. If he had come back I wouldn't have to be here.

But here I am.

There are nicer places to get rid of babies I am sure, but I don't know of any as I ain't in the habit of doing this, and I don't know anybody I could ask who wouldn't want to know why I was asking and all. For sure, I couldn't ask Tish, not that Tish herself would know, God-fearing woman that she is, but I'm sure that crazy Cybil has done this before and Tish is sure to know all the details to pass on. The thing is that Tish has a nose like a basset for sniffing out a secret and I'm just a little innocent hare when it comes to keeping them. It ain't hard to figure out what woulda happened if I had been so stupid as to ask Tish. Tish will sell out on her own mother if the juice is good enough.

This here ain't really a nice place. It is one of those free places they advertise in the classified. All white linoleum and "No Gum, No Mobiles, No Pets, No Food" signs and a metal detector to come in and go out and pamphlets in weird languages that look like drawings for people who don't speak English and probably ain't legal and need to have things done to their parts like everybody else.

Everybody in here is younger than me. Bar none ain't one of them over forty and most of them a lot younger than that, I'd bet, and here I am pushing fifty-five. Everybody either look depressed or indifferent, which sometimes is just a few truck-stops past depressed, anyways. And nobody, save me, ain't seem to care to look at anybody else, and the ones

I looking at either look like they ready to box me down for looking their way or they just ain't meeting my eyes. Lord, come for your world! Arlen always say, "It's a dangerous man that can't look you in the eye", so after a while I just stop looking. At least, not so they can see me.

When I came in here I knew a lot of them probably thought I was lost. Look, they musta been thinking, poor old girl missed the turn for geriatrics, probably need to get her ticker checked *and* fix her cataracts. When I went and gave my name in to the nurse (little Hispanic girl like the one next door my husband calls Chiquita Banana – don't ask me why, that's just Arlen – but Chiquita have three children of her own while this one still got her own mother's milk on her face). Anyway, Chiquita looked at me like she was wondering which patient I was waiting for. And in a way I *have* been sitting here waiting for something other than getting my name called. Like I couldn't possibly be waiting for any of their free attention. I mean, you could blush just looking at some of the posters they hung up in here advertising all the itches and bumps and private maladies you wouldn't discuss with your mother. I mean, there was this one time I thought Arlen had given me something other than just good loving and I itched and avoided him for nearly a week before he could milk it out of me that something wasn't right with the promised land, which is what we called it. Turned out it was just a little yeast, but I was just a teenager and in my day you didn't discuss your privates. And truth be told, I still don't. I mean, there must be a reason why people refer to them that way. Nobody been seeing the promised land but me, Arlen and Dr. Penner at the clinic every year for my check-up, and more often when I had the kids. And only Dr. Penner ever wanted to talk about it. After he checked all the things I didn't have hidden, he would say, "Everything all right down there Detta?" and I'd say, "Right as rain" and he would write on

142

his chart and that would be it. And when I went because me and Arlen had made another baby or I needed a smear or something he would say, "Ok Ms. Adams, everything off from the waist down", and he'd hand me a sheet and look everywhere but there while he got ready and then he'd stare at it and do his thing and try to talk about the weather. And all the time I'd be thinking, "*Ten*, you can, *Nine*, still call, *eight*, me Detta, Dr. Penner, even when, *seven*, you are looking at my parts, *six*, after all it's only me, you, Arlen and the Good Lord, *five*, that ever seen *this* promised land so we might as well, *four*, be familiar…" and by the time I got to two he'd be finished and I could be Detta again, a woman with secrets between her legs.

Stupid as it sounds I think I am more nervous about that than the other part. The very thought of opening up to someone I don't even know, especially if it is some man young enough to be my grandson, is just about enough to make me pass out right here on the damn linoleum. And I absolutely cannot pass out cause that would mean that Chiquita would have to go in my purse and find Arlen's number and call him and say, "Sir, we found a card saying that you are the husband and next of kin of Odetta Adams and we would like you to come on down to the Janis Jay Memorial Women's Reproductive Health Centre and get her cause she just passed out on our linoleum," and Arlen would say, "Well you people musta made one of your crazy mix-up mistakes that I seen on the TV cause my Detta is down at Wong's Waikiki Nails on 23rd & Fulton having her tips done," and Chiquita would say, "No sir, she is surely here and she just passed out and we have therefore decided to postpone her procedure for today," and Arlen will say, "What procedure?" and Chiquita will say talk to me and Arlen will come and then, after he has made sure I am alright, he will start the cotton-picking mind speech, and we know how it will go on but not how it will end, cause after thirty-two years I can't say what he might do if I told him. So I am mostly trying not to think about any of it.

OK Detts, I am telling myself, by this time tomorrow all this is gonna be over and done with and you'll be a free woman and nobody will be any the wiser. Excepting maybe you, of course. You will know to make Arlen cover his stuff up – even if you are almost through the change. You will know to tell Arlen where to get off because you just do not feel like chasing youth again tonight, and a man his age should be getting tired of all that stuff anyway. Same thing I did when I was having the kids. Pain twisting me something terrible, and all I'm doing is holding onto the side of the bed and saying, "OK Detts, by this time tomorrow all this is gonna be over and done with and you will have a beautiful baby to show for it. A little Arlen or Detta to put into the crib that Arlen been fixing up, and to fill out all that knitting and sewing you been doing the past few months." And that pretty much got me through it. Pretty much.

Only this time the pain will not be over this time tomorrow and there will be nothing and no one to show for it.

There are these two girls beside me, still young enough to be sniggering at the diagrams and the pamphlets. One has her mobile plugged into an electrical socket and they are both chewing gum just as loud as can be, smacking bubbles and rolling their eyes. I swear I could slap them into tomorrow just for the gum, besides the fact that they making me all edgy. "Simone, I was, like OH MY GOD!" one is saying. Her mother probably ain't got a clue where Simone is now and probably ain't had a clue where she was when she was doing whatever it is that brought her here in the first place. And then Chiquita says, "Simone Vasquez", like she ain't up for any crap today and Simone takes her time in getting her stuff together, and Chiquita says it again and this time she sounds like she had razors for breakfast

144

and Simone is up and styling over, but not before she make a face at her friend, who stick her tongue out and answer her cellular all at the same time.

I didn't go to Dr. Penner to find out if I was carrying another one of Arlen's babies or not. I just went to a drugstore and bought me a test and put it at the bottom of the basket with a lot of un-necessaries like Kodak film and Vitamin E and rice-cakes – which nobody in my house has ever eaten, and certainly not at my hands, but they hid the test just fine. It was a day I had told Arlen I wanted a ride into town for a new dress just cause I knew he was gonna complain about having to wait for me while I tried every-thing on, and I knew he was eventually gonna get around to asking "Why you gotta get a new dress, though?" and I was gonna give him the evil eye and then he was gonna ask me if I mind if he went to play bid whist with some of the guys at the rec centre until I was done, and I'd tell him go on ahead, a little bit sharp – so it'd sound like I was real upset but not enough for him to decide not to go or nothing. Anyways, I went into the department store and I found me a bathroom and squatted over a stick and I almost missed the window too (what an old girl like me know about aiming?) until I shocked myself so much I almost forgot I had to buy me a dress to come home to Arlen with. I ain't never really expected no two pink lines. I don't even know why I bought the damn test excepting that, though I had been hot-flashing and bleeding and not bleeding on and off for six months almost, I almost always get a particular feeling in me when one of Arlen's little suckers hit the jackpot and a particular pain in my stomach and a particular headachiness and tiredness all at the same time. And I had all those things, and though I did say, "Well, I'll be damned if this change of life thing don't feel just like my time with Janey" (my eldest), I also said, "Detta, you'd better get you one of them stick tests just to be sure you ain't still doing things" – especially cause

145

I remembered that Arlen was particularly loving after that mower me and the kids got him last month for his birthday, and it being his birthday and all I let him have it every night for a whole week. I ain't pretending I didn't like it just as much as he did. Just I'm more disposed to letting him see how much I do sometimes more than others.

Anyway, two pink lines on that sucker and I dropped it like I was branded. Went and bought me another one. More rice-cakes, more Kodak, and some Clairol hair colour that I could use. Same result. Almost forgot my rice-cakes in the toilet stall, washed my hands with the shampoo and rinsed them under the dryer and spent a full ten minutes trying to figure out which end of the tampon dispenser let out the air you dry your hands with.

Went home and fed Arlen rice-cakes for a week while I thought about things – and now here I am.

I mean, it ain't like I ain't thought of alternatives, you know. I thought about making me some canapés with those rice cakes and gathering all the family one evening when Janey didn't have to work late and giving it to them straight – no chaser.

"Latavia," I could have told my middle girl, "don't throw out your maternity clothes girl – I'm gonna need them in a few months."

I could see the girl-kids falling off whatever they had perched on to hear my news. Girl-babies never like the proof that their parents is doing it, especially when they doing it themselves and they think their parents is way too old and over-the-hill for all that. Why, I remember when Janey came and told me she was expecting. I said, "Well I'll be damned if Coslow (that's her husband) ain't shooting him some potent stuff – you all ain't even been married three months." And she be protesting, "Aw, Ma-a-a-a," and I said, "Child, ma is for sheep, you'd better get you some good loving from that man now, while that baby is inside, cause when he get out you ain't gonna have the time or the feeling for that stuff." And she near fainted away herself.

That's how the girl-babies would take it. The boy babies is only two, but Trevor so quiet he probably just nod and tell Arlen congratulations and Anstey couldn't care less once Arlen had put out some brandy and he was close to it.

I could see Arlen grinning that same grin he done grinned the six times I gave him that kinda news before. But I don't know if he woulda grinned it really. I mean, we been fixing to take his retirement money and fly the coop to one of those gated communities in Florida where the cold can't fret his arthritis so much and I could wear those leisure suits made out of terry-towel with the dolphins and the anchors embroidered on them. We had cruises planned and days Arlen would spend riding up and down our lawn in his mower and nights with neighbours over called Sophie and Pete, and barbecue and bridge. Nowhere in there did we plan baby. And after having done had six already, what would I do with another one? If carrying it didn't wreck me, pushing it out surely would. When you been spending some days thinking of ways to save the little energy you have for the things you still have to do in the years you have left, it just don't seem possible to save some for a baby. And what about if Latavia brought hers over for me to babysit. What was I going to tell it, "Oh, hi, Leonard, say hi to your uncle Arlen Jr." and mess up that poor little baby cause he would be thinking: "How he my uncle and he younger than me, though?"

So here I am.

After thirty-two years of marriage, six children and more years on the planet than a good few of the people in here put together.

"Odetta Adams?"

Chiquita look like she been waiting a few minutes while I been dreaming and she holds the door open the few minutes it takes me to get to her. I follow her through weighing-in and temperature-taking and pressure-measuring and peeing in a cup and then I am in a room alone, getting ready to strip and put on a white gown that's gonna expose both the promised land and my wrinkly behind.

The doctor is a woman who could be older than I am. She don't look surprised and she don't mention my age. She just wanna know if somebody is there with me, to take me home. I shake my head cause I will cry if I speak (the hormones, maybe) and she says, that's alright, they will take good care of me until I am steady enough to go home. There is a recovery room I can have for myself after. When she asks, I say I am as ready as I will ever be and they wheel me into another room and another doctor is there sitting by my head and he is a man and I ask him if he gonna stay right there for the whole thing and he say, "Yes mam, I will," and I am thinking, "Thank you, Jesus, he is gonna be at my head and he does not have to see the promised land", and he gives me one little needle and he says he need me to count backwards for him from a hundred just as loud as I can, and when I start he say it don't have to be that loud, and the other doctor and the nurses is laughing and then I think about Arlen and I hope that if he ever find out about all this, if I ever tell him, that he know it wasn't because I ain't love him.

Delores kept losing pieces of herself. Small pieces, at first, with petty agonies. Larger chunks as things progressively worsened. Like the day that she got passed over yet again for the supervisory position (she was sure that she was being discriminated against because she was not yet a citizen) she lost her ability to make small talk in the lunchroom. All the tiny friendly words like "Hi!" and "How are ya!" that Delores had previously used with abandon were swallowed and the ones that marched readily to her tongue when she was faced with her co-workers at the coffee-machine (citizens all) were not fit to be spoken. Certainly not by Delores. So she chewed on expletives and said nothing at all.

On Thursday, Delores arrived home to find that her dog Tobago had run too close to a car-wheel – despite her previous warnings – and died. With his death she lost her ability to make her manager's coffee. On Friday, Delores's best and only friend Jenni decided to take her sari-draped body back to India, the ancestral home that she had never seen. On that day Delores lost her ability to tell the time. The office clock registered no sentiment with her. She arrived at work late every morning, forgot her boss's appointment schedule and stared into space for hours that passed, for her, like mere nanoseconds.

After a week without these lost parts, Delores's grandmother called to say that Samuel Green, her beloved stepfather and her father's murderer, had finally been released from prison after ten years of incarceration and, after expressing a wish to travel to America and visit his step-children, had had a heart-attack and died.

With that, Delores lost her typing speed of 60 words per minute (down to ten words), her love of pastel blue (which induced a particularly draining retching and nausea) and her ability to drive the company pick-up on errands (two unnecessary accidents, a few days apart, both her fault because she no longer knew what the various street signs meant).

On Tuesday Delores got a verbal warning for her persist-ent lateness, a written warning for her snail's pace typing, an invoice for the repairs to the company vehicle and the threat of immediate dismissal for any further infractions in the near future.

And then Delores lost herself altogether.

★　★　★

I had finished being Delores, so I didn't look up from my Snickers when my boss buzzed Delores to take dictation. His buzzing was erratic by the time I swallowed the last bit of caramel and brushed the peanuts off the keyboard.

"Delores. . ." he began in that tone that was saying, "Don'tyourememberthatlittletalkwehadyesterday.Iamwarning you..."

"Mapusa," I corrected him, "Queen of the Sahara Mapusas, of the tribe of Pasi-Pasi, women of the broad forehead and the tiny lower lip, the big bones and feet, sister of she of the quiet left hand, child of Africa, proud mother of modern civilization."

"I am sure," said my boss, "and this is an *urgent* letter to Tony Viera, Managing Director of Viera Associates, he of the large Accounts Receivable, the man with the money. 'Dear Sir' is standard."

My boss was a man of limited understanding.

Delores would never have lifted her head to tell him. But Mapusa did. She borrowed the office scissors which Delores had astutely marked "Administration" with a black permanent marker and started cutting off the dead strands of her relaxed hair.

"Mapusa Tiye has natural hair," I told him, "and no make-up that is not the hand-mixed marking of occasion. . . "

I was systematically removing Delores' faux-pearl dew-drop earrings, her pink plastic Mouseketeer watch, her off-white stockings, and made-in-Taiwan white pointy-toed shoes from the last Payless sale. With my bare palms I erased the frost from her face and looked bare-lipped at my boss's anger through the door that divided us.

"Natural jewellery made of the tooth of the tiger, the tusk of the elephant, the hide of the cow. In Africa we tell the time by the sun and we do not torture our feet with high-heeled shoes. Do you know what those things do to your arches?" I asked him.

My boss was pointing at the door that led out of Administration. There was a sudden absence of the buzz and whine of commercial machinery as the office watched Delores's unravelling.

"Pick up your pink slip at payroll," he said. "You are fired."

Delores would have been embarrassed by the stares of her co-workers but Mapusa was screaming, "Well I wouldn't work here for all the gold in Africa!"

"Well, Delores had no problem with it for the past two years. . ." my boss grunted.

My boss was dialling for a replacement; the newly promoted Supervisor of Administration was calling for security over the office intercom.

It was as if I watched from above as two guards came to pack Delores's things into a cardboard box, one holding her hand uncertainly as if to lead her out of herself. He did not want to treat her roughly. Everyone liked Delores. She had a kind word for everybody.

But I knew Delores was just a fat, quiet and privately weepy bonafide do-gooder of the self-deprecating variety. Miss frumpy-full-of-ordinary-days. And look where it got her.

Delores's memory was staring at me from the mirror tiles in the lobby when the guards led her out and the elevator-doors closed behind her. I surrendered her company ID at the desk and lifted up her box.

"Miss Delores," observed Patrick, the lobby guard, "you cannot walk outside in the road in your bare feet. Would you like me to call you a cab?"

"Mapusa," I correct him, "and in Africa, we walk long distances in our naked feet."

Simone Green had travelled to America with her sister when she was twenty years old, just four years after her stepdad was sent to prison for the murder of her father. Samuel Green was a good man who had rescued a woman and her two daughters from the truth of their lives and given them his name. But he could not rescue them from their past, which turned up, unannounced, on their doorstep one day when sixteen-year-old Simone was practising lines for the school play.

There stood her father.

He had a shotgun.

He had run off eight years before that and they thought he was dead. The Lord's work, her grandmother had said. The man was such a philandering drunkard. With two daughters of his own that he should not want to see treated the way he treated his women. Sins of the father and all that. She was glad to see the back of him and they should be. And life went back to normal for a while without speaking to or about him.

And then there he was.

Simone was stuck on "What are we doing here?" She had been imagining herself two weeks hence, performing on the stage. She and her boyfriend would have run away and gotten lost and she would be saying that to Julian Slater and waiting for the applause for young people able to demonstrate the right decisions on stage to all the parents and her friends and peers. But she was repeating the same line, over and over, to her father. And he wasn't hearing it. Her mother came running. There was an exclamation. And a shot. Her sister ran out. There was another shot. And her sister's hand exploded and shed its fingers at her feet.

Her mother lay dead on the floor.

"What are we doing here? What are we doing here? What are we doing here?" she kept saying as she watched her father turn and leave.

Samuel Green came home to the sympathy of the neighbours and the body of his dead woman and the equally rigid ones of his stepdaughters. So Samuel Green put them both in the back of his pick-up and took them to the hospital where he left them with their grandmother, who fell silent when she saw the look in his eyes. Then Samuel Green drove to every bar on the way out of town until he found her father and murdered him with an ice-pick. The papers said he stabbed him 52 times.

Samuel Green was sentenced to ten years in prison. People said he was lucky. He did not feel lucky. His younger stepchild was disfigured. Friends who were a figment of her childhood imagination never left her, though one by one they moved away so that she never saw them face to face. But she spoke to them all by telephone. Simone had no visible scars from her childhood.

They ditched Samuel's name and flew to America at their grandmother's insistence, leaving the old woman wringing her hands, chanting her rosary and carving bits of her meagre monthly pension for their foreign upkeep. In America, the girls stayed in a hostel and slept in the same bed, pushed up against the wall, scooped together with their backs to the world and their faces to the wall. In America, they struggled to understand how their very presence was against the law and trod quietly in dark places to escape being sent back to the land where they were known by the name of their father's killer.

And when their grandmother sold her wedding band and the silver tea service to buy passports that promised them legitimacy if they became Isabelle Smith and Dianne Smith, they trod quietly because they knew no other way to travel.

Isabelle had been a stripper. Her trademark had been a feather bikini, large loud jewellery and gluteal dexterity. Isabelle went to war every night on top of a bar table in her painted mask and a wide red smile.

⋆　⋆　⋆

"But what will we do now?" asks my sister (she has always been Dianne). "I do not work and we have rent to pay."

She is holding the telephone receiver in her good right hand. The remnant of the other is propped on the dining table, where it sleeps unmoving.

She looks suspiciously at my bare feet, dusty from the highway, Delores's absent watch, her missing make-up, the new hair.

"Oh, Christ, you haven't changed again, have you?"

She sucks her horse teeth before she sets them on her fingernails, which are black-rimmed from the constant onslaught of her molars.

"Oh, my God!" she tells the telephone. "She done gone off again! I am so tired of her crazy ass."

"In Africa," I warn her, "I could have you beheaded for talking to me that way."

154

"Sweet Jesus H. Christ!!!" screeches my sister. "Don't bother! I going starve now and die anyway!"

She spits nails at my feet.

On Friday, my sister is mumbling into the telephone again. Her lips almost cover the part of the receiver not smothered by her good fist.

"Schizophrenicdysfunctionalobesecrazyassedchocolate scarfingfreak!" she is saying and her voice is climbing with each insult and tightening her grip on the phone until she is screaming and her knuckles are white. She is not looking at me. She has tried not to since I became Mapusa. I am eating milk chocolate so sweet each swallow sears my throat and leaves my spittle soothing sugar burns.

We are surrounded by the evidence of Delores's undoing. Her clothing sits in a pile in the middle of the living room floor awaiting a trip to Goodwill. Her touch is missing from the household: she is no longer here to clean the dishes every morning before catching the 7:23 No. 6 to work, cannot leave the sink gleaming as her everyday legacy. She cannot water the houseplants and they have started to wilt from her inattention. Her crochet pieces have been placed underneath the front of the fridge to catch the water that it has bled since the electricity went out. Delores always remembered to charge the key and now that she is gone Mapusa cannot find it.

"It is probably the blasted sugar," my sister tells the telephone. "She cannot stop eating chocolate, you know, and we both know that diabetics sometimes get mental..."

"I am not diabetic," I reply. Delores's insulin and needles sit untouched on our centre table.

I scratch my scalp's new curly fuzz and brush chocolate off the leopard-print skirt I bought with my payment in lieu of notice. It could be mistaken for something Isabelle might have worn, but it is long so I do not worry. I wonder if they have this brand of chocolate in Africa. I cannot remember but I am sure we were probably the first to find joy in the cocoa bean.

In the newspaper I scan the classifieds.

When I was Isabelle I worked in a bar, shedding my clothes each night like old skin and shivering on purpose, for money. One night, one of the regulars waited for me in the alley beside the bar, grabbed me from behind, dragged me deeper into darkness and said he needed to touch my shaking ass to see if it was real. His touch shattered my name, branded my skin and scared me shitless. At the end of it Isabelle lay crying in the alley, trying to force herself to breathe.

And I became Delores.

Delores was too fat to shimmy up and down a fire pole so she typed.

Mapusa will do neither.

★　★　★

"Your references do not seem to remember who you are," says Mr. Brown, who is actually pink and is dressed in blue. Silk, I think. Or a very real-looking synthetic blend. His little finger is perpetually at right angles to the rest of his hand. On it he wears a diamond-encrusted pinky ring. His shoes are white. He walks with a swagger and says "dahling" regularly.

"I am sure they don't," I say, in between bites of a peppermint centre. "There are many more whom colonialism has made forgetful."

"Luckily for you, dahling," he continues, "this is not a popular position, nor is it rocket science."

He is from the Southern US, perhaps, but he does not look as if he belongs in heat. His office is white as snow. His face is powdered white. I suspect his eyelashes were purchased at a very sweet-smelling department store. He does not appear to sweat, although his hanky is never too far from his brow.

156

He reaches across his desk to lift my chin and looks hard at me, as if he is trying to see beneath my skin. As if he cannot decide what to make of me. I am steadily eating my chocolate.

"I don't know your real story, dahling," he begins, "but if you do your job I don't have to. Seven dollars an hour." He comes around to the front of his desk and looks at my feet.

"And you will wear shoes in deference to the dearly departed."

I begin to object but he lifts a snowy finger to his lips.

"Dahling," he says, "you simply *must*."

I can hardly sleep for all the muttering my sister is making into the phone on her side of our bed.

"The frigging psycho freak now dressing damn dead people and TOUCHING MY BREAD!"

She is yelling.

"I wash my hands before I come home," I respond.

Her legs are drawn up beneath her. She has placed a pillow between herself and the wall she is facing. As usual her back is spooned into my chest. Wind cannot blow between us.

"She smells of the dead," my sister whispers. "The smell is everywhere." And then my sister starts to cry.

I do not know what to say.

"They are just like us, Dianne," I say. "Just sleeping. How would you like it if I refused to touch you just because you could not talk to me?"

"I can talk to you!" says Dianne.

It is the first time she has spoken to me directly since Samuel Green. She turns towards me and we hug, both of us crying.

We bury Delores's clothing and her crochet in a trash bin we find on the street. We put her to rest with Isabelle's bikinis. My sister spray-paints the wall behind the can with her good hand and the hiss of the spray is soothing. When she is done it says: "Here lie two special women. Rest In Peace."

At work there is a funeral.

I have encircled the coffin with ascending bouquets of carnations and roses. I have provided the pre-recorded inspirational tunes Mr. Brown orders from glossy catalogues with pictures of cascading waterfalls and trees and swans on lakes. I have opened the guest-book at the door and secured it on a brass lectern with brass scrollwork. I have stacked up prayer cards that say "Thank you for your kindness and sympathy on this sad occasion" for ushers to distribute.

Last night I applied face powder and a hint of brown lipstick. Mr. Brown had me reverse the hearse to the door of the chapel to await the coffin after the guests have paid their last respects.

The relatives come first and an old woman christens the wreaths with the first tears. She is feeble and gasping. I hold her shaking hand and guide her up the flowers until we reach the casket. She cries on my starch-perfect pressing and my immaculate make-up and touches my carefully wrapped head-scarf. When she is finished I am ready with a tissue and one of eighty-six folding chairs I arranged myself.

I ask her if she wants a glass of water.

"Who are you?" she asks, as if she has seen me for the first time.

"Mapusa Tiye," I reply. "Queen of the Sahara Nomad Tiyes of the tribe of Pasi-Pasi, we of the broad forehead and the tiny lower lip, the big bones and feet, child of Africa and sister of she of the quiet left hand, proud mother of modern civilization."

Her eyes widen.

"Who?" she repeats, and her breath stirs the dust on the surface of the tissue frozen in her suspended left hand.

ABOUT THE AUTHOR

Cherie S A Jones was born in 1974. She received a LL.B degree from the University of the West Indies, Barbados, in 1995, a Legal Education Certificate from the Hugh Wooding Law School, St Augustine, Trinidad in 1997 and was admitted to the Bar in Barbados in October 1997. While studying at the University of the West Indies she was an active member of the Creative Writer's Society. In 1992 she was awarded the first runner-up prize in the local leg of the First Ladies of the Americas Creative Writing Competition. Her story 'Bride' was the winner of the first prize in the 1999 Commonwealth Short Story Competition and a prize of £2,000. She lives in Barbados.

OTHER SHORT STORY COLLECTIONS YOU MIGHT LIKE

Hazel Campbell, *Singerman*, 0-948833-44-0, £6.99
Realistic and magical, sombre and comic, heroic and ironic, these stories
explore Jamaican reality through a variety of voices and forms, connecting
the slave past and contemporary gang warfare.

Kwame Dawes, *A Place to Hide*, 1-900715-48-1, £9.99
Dawes's characters are driven by their need for intimate contact: with
people, with God, with their creative potential. Their stories give an incisive
portrayal of contemporary Jamaica that is unsparing in confronting its
elements of misogyny & violence.

Meiling Jin, *Song of the Boatwoman*, 0-948833-86-6, £6.95
These stories, set in Guyana, London, America, Malaysia and China, explore
the inner lives of women of the Chinese diaspora, lesbian sexuality and
racism.

Rabindranath Maharaj, *The Writer and his Wife*, 0-948833-81-5, £7.99
Maharaj's Trinidadian characters struggle heroically, though sometimes
comically, to make their mark on the earth. It is as if the more frustrating their
outward circumstances, the more intense their inner lives.

E.A. Markham, *Taking the Drawing Room Through Customs*, 1-900715-69-4, £9.99
Whether writing with observant humour, occasional bleakness, audacious
mythologising or absurdist magical realism, the crafted completeness of the
stories in this collection reveal Markham as a master of the short story form.

Geoffrey Philp, *Uncle Obadiah and the Alien*, 1-900715-01-5, £6.99
Drawing on rasta and ragamuffin flavours, science fiction and tall tales, these
short stories set in Jamaica and Miami have humour and pathos in their explora-
tions of families, race, class and sexual orientation.

N.D. Williams, *Julie Mango*, 1-900715-77-5, £9.99
Williams's characters want the space to cultivate their sense of individual
worth, though this can sometimes involve becoming trapped in an absurd or
confining persona. At the heart of all the stories is the plea for a humane
tolerance.

All Peepal Tree titles are available from our website:
www.peepaltreepress.com

Explore our list of over 160 titles, read sample poems and reviews,
discover new authors, established names and access a wealth of
information about books, authors and Caribbean writing. Secure
credit card ordering, fast delivery throughout the world at cost or
less.

You can contact us at:
Peepal Tree Press, 17 King's Avenue, Leeds LS6 1QS, United Kingdom
Tel: +44 (0) 113 2451703 E-mail: hannah@peepaltreepress.com